The SWEET FOLLY of HOPE

a novel

KATHERINE H. BROWN

First Stillwater River Publications Edition

ISBN: 978-1-963296-24-2

Library of Congress Control Number: 2024903010

Names: Brown, Katherine H. (Katherine Houston), author.
Title: The sweet folly of hope : a novel / Katherine H. Brown.
Description: First Stillwater River Publications edition. | West Warwick, RI, USA : Stillwater River Publications, [2024]
Identifiers: ISBN: 978-1-963296-24-2 (paperback) | LCCN: 2024903010
Subjects: LCSH: City dwellers--California--San Francisco--Fiction. | Community gardens--California--San Francisco--Fiction. | Real estate developers--California--San Francisco--Fiction. | Families--Fiction. | Friendship--Fiction. | Self-actualization (Psychology)--Fiction. | Communities--Fiction.
Classification: LCC: PS3602.R7217 S94 2024 | DDC: 813/.6--dc23

1 2 3 4 5 6 7 8 9 10

Written by Katherine H. Brown.
Cover design by Matt St. Jean.
Interior design by Elisha Gillette.
Permissions for poems granted by their respective authors.
Published by Stillwater River Publications, West Warwick, RI, USA.

The views and opinions expressed in this book are solely those of the author(s) and do not necessarily reflect the views and opinions of the publisher.

To my granddaughters, Sophia and Samantha.

CONTENTS

SPRING

How surely gravity's law,
strong as an ocean current,
takes hold of even the smallest thing
and pulls it toward the heart of the world.

Rainer Maria Rilke. *Rilke's Book of Hours. Love Poems to God.* Translated by Anita Barrows and Joanna Macy. New York: Riverhead Books. 1996.

LOTTE

"No stinky cabbages in my garden. N-o-p-e. N-o-p-e. N-o-p-e."

Across the mess of seed packages, paper cups, and potting soil covering her dining room table, Lotte chuckled good-naturedly at the loud "p" Allegra popped with her lips. But when Allegra followed by sticking out her tongue in a taunt, Lotte inhaled deeply and counted to ten to buy time before responding. She dodged eye contact with the child's glare and let her thoughts drift happily instead to the sleeping garden in a vacant lot three floors below her loft in San Francisco's Mission District.

Smiling, she summoned a picture of a sun-bright day with friends and families, their gladness welling up from a tumble of flowers and vegetables. As always, the hopes that came with this vision heartened her. Not only hope, but a growing conviction that the garden could mend her own fragmented family—and, perhaps, also bring healing to others in the neighborhood. Once strangers, the gardeners who were working with Lotte also seemed to seek a safe place in the turbulent world around them. Together, their cleanup efforts over the past weeks were actually beginning to show results—enough, at least, for Lotte that evening to teach Allegra how to start seeds indoors in anticipation of planting them in their future garden.

An empty paper cup sailed by Lotte's head, interrupting her pleasant musings. As the cup fell behind her, it made a light tap on the wooden floor. She raised her eyebrows, once more amused by the sight of Allegra's face, now puckered into a pout. Apparently proud of her aeronautic feat, the child wiped her hands on the dirt-smudged bib of her new corduroy overalls, shoved up the sleeves of her pink sweater with its bear-shaped pearl buttons, and put her hands on her hips. *Proud?* wondered Lotte. *Or fixing for a fight?*

Lotte wasn't sure. She'd brought Allegra—her granddaughter by circumstance, not birth—from New York only three weeks earlier, when Liz, Allegra's mother, checked herself into an alcohol treatment center. Since that harrowing day, Lotte had witnessed Allegra's volatility many times. She was enchanting one moment and explosive the next.

Conscious that she risked triggering a full-blown tantrum, Lotte opted to hold firm—not so much in defense of the vegetable, but more importantly for Allegra's sake. She gently asserted her authority as the adult in the room.

"Yes, indeed we will plant cabbage. Cabbage moths and bunnies love it, even if you don't."

"Bunnies don't live in the city," sassed back Allegra. "They need grass and holes in the ground, stupid."

Bifocals balanced at the end of her nose, Lotte ignored the insult, smiled at Allegra's frown, and answered, "Don't be so sure. Gardens have a way of bringing all kinds of life, not just bunnies, to the city. Wait and see. You're in for a surprise, little Ladybug."

Lotte glanced to check Allegra's reaction. Sometimes the child enjoyed her affectionate nicknames, but other times she took offense. In this instance, Allegra seemed determined to show no sign of hearing her at all as she mutely placed a tiny seed into the soil she'd packed into a paper cup. Lotte noted with silent gratification that Allegra covered the seed tenderly with a dusting of soil, exactly as she'd shown her to do.

"Harrumph," grumped Allegra, plunking the cup onto the tray where others like it were arranged. "There's your cabbage for your bunnies."

"Thank you," answered Lotte, acknowledging Allegra's gesture as a peace offering. In turn, she offered her own gift. "There's a poem you may like. It's by Wendell Berry, a farmer, and it goes like this…'Sowing the seed, my hand is one with the earth…'"

"Mines are two with the earth," interrupted Allegra. Giggling, she held up two muddy palms.

"For sowing the cabbage seed and for those two cute little gardener's hands, the bunnies and I thank you, Miss Princess Potter."

Allegra's laughter washed over Lotte like balm, easing slightly the knot that had lodged between her shoulders since taking on the daily juggle of Allegra's needs. With her busy life as a freelance writer, she'd known it wouldn't be all roses by any stretch, and likely would only get worse in a few weeks when Liz also moved in with them, newly sober.

Lotte bit her lower lip. The timing couldn't be worse. A looming deadline for the prestigious magazine *Orion* fell two days after Liz's expected arrival. It was a huge honor to be invited by the magazine's editors to add a cultural perspective for their issue on secrecy and lies. *Damn*, thought Lotte irritably. *When am I supposed to write?*

"How come Mom hated Gran?"

"Where'd that come from?" answered Lotte, jolted from her deadline angst by Allegra's non sequitur. Cautiously curious, she leaned in to give Allegra her full attention while at the same time bracing herself, fully aware of Allegra's instinct to direct their conversations into troublesome terrain.

Allegra shrugged. "'Cause you're not my real Gran."

The words wounded. How Lotte wished Allegra wouldn't push her away from the very role she longed to fill, a place she felt entitled and more than deserving to claim. Hadn't she done everything in her power to forge a connection with Liz from the start when she moved in with Vince, her then-boyfriend and Liz's father? Putting up with the cyclone moodiness of a teenager was more than Lotte bargained for, but family for Lotte meant sticking together through thick and thin. So, of course, later she took in Liz when she appeared bedraggled and pregnant on her doorstep, only months after Lotte had bid good riddance to Vince. She'd been there for Allegra's birth, too, and afterward. Happily, she changed diapers, baby-proofed the loft, and unflaggingly bolstered Liz into motherhood and the start of a singing career. When Liz and Allegra moved east, Lotte helped as much as she could from afar. She felt wretched, unable to save Liz from her progressively noticeable slide into alcoholism, but she dropped everything when Liz, mired in shame and fearful for Allegra, turned to Lotte for help, again.

Who needs this grandmother role, anyway? Lotte bristled internally, whipped up by resentments she thought were long passed, but obviously were not. In the past week she'd had to cancel a date with friends to see Olu Dara at Yoshi's jazz club in Oakland, an NAACP-SF board meeting, and a one-off, easy, but high-paying interview with a young woman running for attorney general. She'd washed and folded more laundry than she usually did in a month, and gone daily to the grocery store to buy food for meals the child refused to eat. Who asked for this trouble? Lotte firmly folded her arms across her chest. *Fine*, she resolved silently, *You're right. I am not your Gran, or anyone else's for that matter. You and your mother, be damned.*

Instantly, Lotte regretted this unspoken flash of annoyance toward the vulnerable little girl before her. Sure, Allegra's misplaced anger and sly, five-year-old charm had at times been a trial, but with no living relatives, Liz and Allegra were her only family. For all the trouble they were, the truth was…Liz and Allegra meant more to Lotte than she dared to think.

She relaxed her arms and leaned forward, replying genuinely, "Well, I feel like I'm your real Grandma, child."

"Nope. You're not."

Ouch. Lotte flinched again despite herself as Allegra continued, seemingly oblivious to the hurtful effect she was having.

"My Gran's dead. She died when Mom was a little

baby. But it's okay, Lotte. I promised Mom I'd be a Big Girl, and Big Girls don't need grandmothers. They don't need nobody."

Poor, dear Allegra. Lotte's heart ached as she listened to the child's transparent bravado and watched her scrawl a forlorn looking cat with her finger in the spilled soil on the table. Fathomless pain lay beneath Allegra's Big Girl defense.

"Maybe…Mom's mad at Gran and not at me, huh?"

"That well could be," answered Lotte, astonished not for the first time by Allegra's capacity for flip-flopping between swagger and emotional insight. "Why don't you ask her?"

"Nope. No way." Allegra wiped away the cat and replaced it with a wobbly sketch of a smiley face.

Lotte registered how their conversation had inadvertently stumbled upon an idea she'd been exploring for her *Orion* article, how masking one's anger can be a form of lying which, if unexamined and not chosen, might be harmful to the person, their family, and even society. She wondered whether she could make sense of this for a five-year-old. Perhaps Allegra, no stranger to Liz's angry outbursts or her own childish temper tantrums, might have insights of her own about the issue. Maybe this was a chance to bridge the divide between work and child raising? She decided to give it a try.

"My hunch is that your Mom has mixed-up feelings about her mother and hides them behind a mask…a mask of anger. Does that make sense?"

"Uh-huh," Allegra mumbled and nodded, her furrowed brow telling otherwise.

"Sometimes," Lotte explained, "I can't bear to be angry so I cry instead. Hmmm…? Does that happen to you?"

Allegra shook her head no.

"I don't plan to cry," continued Lotte. "But something inside me is afraid of my anger. Like it will blow everyone—including me and all those I love—away, and get me in trouble. So, most times I cry instead."

Lotte stopped, not sure if she'd gone too far. Would Allegra be afraid to learn of Lotte's anger? Only minutes earlier, hadn't she bitten her tongue to protect the child from her momentary spark of irritation? She found herself wondering where, when, and how it is beneficial to express anger outright. Certainly, as she'd begun to argue in her article, there's rarely merit to suppressing outrage in the face of injustice. For too long, her enslaved forebears had borne untold cruelty, insult, and exclusion, and hidden their smoldering anger for fear of their lives. What cost to them and future generations was this form of brutal psychic repression?

When she felt Allegra's eyes searching her face,

Lotte smiled to reassure her. She switched gears from literary journalist to grandmother and said lightly, "Oh, everybody gets angry sometimes. Yup, even me. What's important is to know what's underneath the anger. Isn't that what matters, hmm…?" She pushed her reading glasses up on her nose and motioned for Allegra to pass a stack of empty cups. "When I was growing up, my mother told me in no uncertain terms that women aren't ever to get angry, let alone show it. So, it felt safer to cry instead. But now that I'm grown, I've learned to recognize my tears are often only a cover-up of anger. Here, let me show you.

"Pretend I'm angry." Lotte grimaced and growled, "GRRRRRR." Then, she sniffled like she was crying and covered her face with her hands. "The anger feels too ugly, and really scary. So I bury it behind my tears.

"And interestingly, it also works the other way, too. Sometimes I feel sad, but don't want anyone to know, so I hide behind an angry mask. Instead of showing tears, I strike out and my temper shows. Maybe that's what's going on with Liz and your Gran. Maybe she seems angry but is really, really sad that her mother died."

Lotte wondered what the child was thinking as Allegra picked up an empty cup and tried pushing the pencil gently through the bottom to make a drainage hole for the seedling. When it wouldn't go through, she pushed harder, forcibly jamming the pencil point until it punctured the cup. In rapid succession, she stabbed holes in three more cups.

"Anger and sadness switch places, sometimes," hurried Lotte, recognizing Allegra's diminishing interest. "It's confusing, but worth thinking about." She scooted her chair back from the table and held her arms wide open, welcoming Allegra. "Hey, my little Fingerling Potato—not to change the subject, but I sure could use some starfish hugs. Hmmm…?"

Upon seeing Allegra jump from her chair and run around the table, the knot between Lotte's shoulders eased once again. When Allegra clambered into her lap, Lotte delighted in the way the child's thin legs clung like long-lost puzzle pieces into the soft niches of her broad waist. She pressed her palms into Allegra's back and nuzzled close into her smell. The child smelled like outside, like rain, like cookies, like Allegra.

"That's right. Belly to belly," Lotte crooned and rocked Allegra side to side in her embrace. "Like the starfish we saw in the aquarium do, pressed up against the rocks so tight no one can pull them apart. That's it. There's my little one, coming back home."

Coming back home? Lotte savored the comfort of her own words. Then, like minnows darting under a bridge away from the danger of open water, her sense of ease vanished instantly with Allegra's plaintive request: "Can we call Mom tonight?"

"You miss her, don't you?"

"No."

Lotte knew this wasn't true. "I'm sure Liz wants to talk to you too, Button Nose. But it's the middle of the night in New York and she's probably asleep. Let's wait until tomorrow when she's going to call us."

She felt Allegra's body relax into her arms and she pulled her closer. When the rise of laughter began in her own belly, Lotte knew exactly what to do. Allegra must have sensed it too, for she was giggling even before Lotte began to tickle her fingers along Allegra's tiny ribs.

They laughed until Lotte caught sight of the clock on the kitchen wall. She sat up straight and, pretending to be alarmed, said in her most no-nonsense voice, "Hey, what's going on? Look at the time! How come you aren't in bed?"

Lotte saw panic in Allegra's eyes and realized the child must not have recognized her make-believe tone. Lotte gently tightened her hold and patted Allegra's back for a time. She knew all was well again when the child slipped out of her grasp and stood tall on the floor in front of her, grinning.

"To beddy-bye with you, Ms. Twiglet," Lotte sang out as Allegra skipped off toward her new bedroom door.

–

Lotte closed the book she'd been reading to Allegra in bed and stood quietly so as not to wake the child. She bent to the sleeping face and kissed her smooth forehead, resisting the urge to run a finger over the sprinkle of freckles dancing across Allegra's nose.

Overcome by a mix of heartache and joy, her breath caught. She hugged her arms for comfort until the feeling passed, then offered a silent prayer. *Brave little Allegra, my sweet happiness, the Buddhas are here. May you sleep well and wake in safety with an open heart.*

Lotte sighed as she stepped back into the center of the loft. Her usually clean and well-organized office desk was covered with piles of coloring books and drawings. Files and research books for "Family Secrets," the article she was writing for *Orion*, were stacked helter-skelter wherever she looked.

The last time she'd sat down to write, she'd left off without knowing where next to take the piece. She was happy with the article's beginning, starting with her family's passed-down story about secretly harboring slaves desperate to reach Canada prior to Emancipation. As free "negroes" working for a Presbyterian minister at Princeton, her family had certain liberties, but they risked everything by providing safe haven without their employer's blessing. Next, she wanted to take the article into the seamier, less obviously heroic side of secrets—the kind that wrench families apart. But she wasn't yet sure how to go about it. She certainly wasn't ready to air her own still-raw personal experience with secrets gone awry.

What she needed was focused time to sort out the article's direction. But time was in scarce reserve since responding to Liz's cry for help. *How will I ever make the deadline?* Lotte's anxious query to no one was swallowed into the night's silence. She made a mental note to call the magazine editor first thing the next morning to beg for an extension, something she prided herself on never doing. And when her eye caught sight of a drawing of a spectacular fire-breathing dragon taped to her computer screen, she vowed to set better limits on Allegra's spillover. But forgiveness followed fast, granted not only to Allegra but also to herself for taking on too much. *Not to worry,* she reasoned, confident the magazine wouldn't hesitate to give her an extra week for a deadline.

Besides, who could resist this array of coloring books and crayons? Or the way Allegra purses her lips when she's concentrating? Shaking her head and amazed at her growing tolerance for disorder, Lotte mused, *I must be in love. I am clearly losing my mind to love.* She bent to pick up a single red sneaker and searched for its match in the open space of the loft.

Eight years earlier, her loft apartment was simply an empty warehouse in the center of San Francisco's Mission District. Once Lotte set her eyes on it, she easily envisioned the potential of a home where morning light and the sounds of the city filtered through its floor-to-ceiling windows. Raw from her break-up with Vince, she immediately pounced upon the chance to use her imprint to turn it into her own special place.

At her direction, a carpenter built walls for two bedrooms along the north side, separated by a shared bathroom. One of these rooms had been intended for a guest room for the company that inevitably passed through town. Liz and Allegra had shared the room for two crowded, tumultuous, but gratifying years before their move to New York, and again it was to be theirs. Lotte was beginning more and more to admit she'd designed the loft for this very purpose.

A small but efficient kitchen took up one end of the south wall. A Ficus tree dominated the window space between the kitchen and her office space. Although her furnishings were simple and spare, she'd taken care to ensure the room offered a comfortable refinement, unspoiled by Allegra's flotsam. Lotte's hand-crafted, oak, round center table, now smothered under potting soil, reminded her of evenings of provocative conversation and good food for which she was well known among her wide circle of friends.

She retrieved the second red sneaker peeking out from under the sofa along the eastern wall and placed both little shoes next to one another on a low table littered with a wild display of playing cards connected to no game Lotte recognized.

Where to start? Her answer came quietly. She crossed the room and stood above a plump Indian-print cushion in the center of a square black pad on the floor. Meditation was vital to the peace she knew she would find within her. Lotte knelt on the cushion and closed her eyes. Shifting slightly, she lifted the cushion to find a worn rag doll underneath; she placed the doll in her lap. They both faced forward and grew quiet together.

Calmness settled in for a moment before thoughts turned to the next day's plan for a garden work party in the neighborhood's community garden. Lotte recalled how for years the vacant lot served as a hangout for people who drifted through the area. Littered with trash, cigarette filters, broken glass, used condoms, needles and the other residue of city life, it had taken weeks for the first neighborhood crew to clean up the mess and make the area safe for everyone. The crew grew, and now it seemed the whole neighborhood showed up daily to give hands-on attention as the garden took shape. Lotte's mind ticked though the items on her to-do list for the next day: thermos, celery and peanut butter snacks, the compost bucket for the garden's worm box, sunscreen, hats, heavy-duty garden gloves, tools and Anne Spencer's poem. Oh, and remember to find a screen for sifting soil...

Mid-list, her attention returned to the cushion beneath her. She gently replaced her focus on her breathing, noting silently the word that described her digression: "planning." The to-do list gave way to the words of her meditation teacher: "Minds get bored, so they run away and we run with them. With practice, we return to our breath and there we find peace. The breath doesn't care; it's patient. It can wait a lifetime for our attention, ten million lifetimes if need be."

She recalled the fraught state she'd been in when she heard these words in the midst of her breakup with Liz's father and Allegra's grandfather. She was shattered when Vince told her he'd fallen for one of his students. It took every inner resource for Lotte to crawl back from that betrayal.

Lotte was drawn to Vince from the first time they met, and despite her friends' doubts to her sanity, she moved from her home in San Francisco to live with him and Liz in Kansas City, where he taught at the university. Weathering the storms of Liz's adolescence and midwestern winters, Lotte was sure she and Vince were in for the long haul. His announcement came as a shock. But when neighbors, gossips, and acquaintances came forward to comfort, too often they revealed other of his dalliances and she knew the relationship could not be fixed.

What a waste. She sighed as her thoughts turned to revisit their good times. Vince was a brilliant man in so many ways. She cherished their companionship, and years later still sometimes ached to wake next to the part of him that shared the tumble of ideas pouring out between them each morning. So handsome, too—the way his auburn beard tinged with gray as their seven-year relationship aged. And sexy. She'd found Vince's seductiveness irresistible, that vulnerable, come-take-care-of-me way he had. His voice, so soft she had to lean in to hear him, made even a grocery list or menu feel intimate.

Memories transported Lotte back to the day they met. His voice, hoarse with laryngitis, was reduced to a whisper. As new board members for the Community Foundation, a progressive foundation in San Francisco, they'd paired up to review several grant proposals together. When the time came to present recommendations Vince pleaded, "Can you take the lead? I can't talk." Lotte was flattered by his confidence and offered to bring her tried-and-true remedy of cayenne, honey, and lemon tea to his hotel room after the meeting.

"Guaranteed for what ails you…if it doesn't kill you first," she promised.

She was startled when Vince met her at the door of his room with a filled champagne glass in hand. Behind him she saw a bellhop lighting candles on a table spread with an elegant dinner for two, and right then, she knew she would stay the night if asked.

She leaned toward him as he whispered, "I've poured myself a glass—a chaser, in case your concoction is as noxious as it sounds."

She liked how he gently led her by the arm. "You'll join me for supper? Hopefully not our last. I'd like it to be the first of many."

"I suspect it won't be our last," Lotte replied with a willing smile.

As if on signal, they met halfway in embrace, their supper growing cold as they warmed each other. How she treasured the whisperings and closeness of that long night, and the many that followed…

Lotte interrupted her memories, acknowledging them as yet another digression from her meditation. She shook off the nostalgia of lost love and returned to the present by shifting her weight on the cushion. Wiping away the traces of anger and sadness, Lotte consciously replaced them with gratitude at the thought of the sleeping child in her apartment. Without Vince there would be no Liz, no Allegra.

ALLEGRA

Allegra woke the next morning thinking about pancakes. Wrapped in her bright red comforter-cape, she peered out of her bedroom door and met Lotte's eyes peeking out above the rim of her coffee mug.

"Good morning, Pigeon."

Allegra stomped barefoot past Lotte to the kitchen. "My feet are cold," she announced.

"And good morning to you, Pigeon," repeated Lotte.

"Good morning," Allegra barked. Ignoring Lotte, she drew up a chair, cleared a patch of room on the table and turned to look at the gray sky out the window. "I hate it here. It's freezing."

"Might try some shoes or slippers, and—"

"NO! I don't want shoes or slippers." Allegra

stamped one foot to emphasize the fact. *Uh-oh,* she thought seeing Lotte raise her eyebrows. *I'm in trouble now.*

She missed her Mom who was still in New York, getting better in what Lotte called a rehab center. She curled her fingers into tight fists, digging her nails into the skin of her palms, a trick she did to keep tears from sneaking out from wherever they live inside. *No tears,* she commanded silently, and marched back into her bedroom, slamming the door.

"Stupid, stupid, stupid," Allegra muttered as she yanked open and emptied all three dresser drawers, scattering T-shirts, pants, shorts, socks, sweaters, and underwear across the floor. From the pile, she picked out a purple turtleneck and carefully matched it with pink overalls and blue socks. She wasn't going to be teased again about being Miss Matchless, like her Mom once called her back home when she was a little girl. Almost six now, she knew better.

"Where are my stupid sneakers?" She kicked her clothes from one place to another and opened the door. "My sneakers are gone," she announced, hands on hips the way she'd seen Lotte do.

"On the table by the sofa, Chickadee," she heard Lotte say from behind the newspaper.

"I am not a bird," grumped Allegra, under her breath so Lotte wouldn't hear her. She pulled on her socks and sock-footed herself across the floor, wedged on her sneakers, and carefully tied their laces.

"How about some hot cereal, Ms. Marshmallow?"

"Is that all there is?" whined Allegra, all hope of pancakes erased. "I hate hot cereal."

"First I heard," came Lotte's reply.

"I'm telling you now," Allegra snapped, then hated herself for being angry with Lotte. She was probably more sad than angry, like Lotte was talking about the night before, but tears were for babies.

"Well, it's what's happening 'round here this morning, so best make do."

Allegra put on her sour face as Lotte placed a steaming bowl of oatmeal on the table in front of her. The hot cereal was slimy, and Lotte only let her put in one spoonful of sugar. She hated that Lotte gave her no choice. Bossy Lotte was boss of sugar and of everything else in this place.

"And some orange juice, and...I don't figure you'll object to...?" asked Lotte.

The sight of tiny marshmallows spreading into a floating pool of sweetness on top of a big mug of hot chocolate melted Allegra's grumpiness all away.

"Fan—*tastic!*"

The last drop of hot chocolate licked clean, Allegra spooned slow circles into the blob of cold oatmeal in front of her and listened to Lotte list their plans for the day.

"First, we pick up this place. A tornado called Allegra has been through here," Lotte said with a wink and a smile. "And then I have to get some work done at my desk until lunch, but after that…"

"Yippee! To the garden and Godfrey," finished Allegra. Feeling thoroughly happy, she swung her heels back and forth under her chair.

"Yup, that's the plan. Our friends Mr. Adams and Mrs. Hatfield will be there. Nina said she and Raul might come too. The fog should have burned off and the sun's gonna shine."

"I love the garden, Lotte." She couldn't wait to find out if Mr. Adams liked her compost bucket, and she wondered if she could show Raul her worm box and whether Mrs. Hatfield would bring her warm cookies.

Out of the corner of her eye, she saw Lotte looking out the window, so she quickly opened the bag, plopped a handful of mini-marshmallows on top of her uneaten cereal, and buried them. Everything was going right.

"It's my favorite place in the whole world."

"The garden's a wonder to everyone, isn't it? Even to the worms," Lotte said. "Want to feed them today?"

"Yes, yes! Hot cereal. Godfrey loves oatmeal." She pushed the cereal away.

"Fat chance, Ms. Pollywog," countered Lotte as she tapped the bowl back in her direction. "The whole caboodle goes into yoodle, or you'll be so hungry the worms will need to watch out you don't eat them."

"Gross! People don't eat worms." *Or do they?* She held her nose and searched carefully for hidden marshmallows, taking a bite here, a bite there, until finally she reached the bottom of the bowl.

LOTTE

fter lunch, Lotte handed a dripping salad plate to Allegra. She watched the child carefully dry and stack it onto others in the dish rack on the counter. With a swipe of sponge, she rinsed the sink, reached down to take up the towel, and dried her hands.

"Thank you. You are such a good helper, Pumpkin."

"You're welcome. I help my mom all the time."

"I'm sure you do," Lotte responded, concealing her concern.

She knew Allegra's eagerness to help was not necessarily a good sign. Much, she suspected, had fallen on this precious child's shoulders as her mother sank deeper into an alcoholic haze. When Liz called Lotte to say she'd hit bottom, though her slurred words were barely coherent, her plea for help was crystal clear. Lotte caught a red-eye flight east and arrived the next morning. Their apartment was a mess, but she watched as Allegra picked up keys, glasses, and clothes that Liz had left lying everywhere in her stupor, as if it were routine. Allegra boasted that she also packed her own lunch for school and made her own dinner. Beyond shock, Lotte was especially saddened to witness Allegra bring aspirin and iced juice to fix her mother's breakfast screwdriver.

Lotte willed these memories away and turned from the sink to admire her now-nearly-neat loft. "Lookin' good, don't you think?"

Hearing no response, she turned back to find Allegra balancing tiptoe on the stool to reach the compost bucket at the back of the sink. Lotte tried to move the bucket closer, but Allegra pushed her hand away.

"I can do it myself," declared Allegra as she pulled the plastic container to the edge of the counter and pried open the lid. "Yuck, it stinks."

"Just as Godfrey likes it," Lotte assured, and squinted into the container full of carrot peelings, eggshells, noodles, and wilted lettuce from their dinner the day before. "Looks like he's got a feast coming to him today."

She lifted a canvas bag loaded with snacks, added a water thermos, and offered to carry the plastic compost container for Allegra.

"Nope. I got it."

Allegra's continual insistence on self-sufficiency seared Lotte's heart, and not for the first time that morning she questioned whether she was up for the ups and downs of being a round-the-clock grand-mother. She caught herself, breathed deeply, and exhaled, knowing the question was answerable only moment to moment.

"Let's go, then. Where's your coat, Meadowlark?"

"In the closet where you put it this morning, dummy."

Lotte's reaction was swift. "Uh-oh. So many words, why choose ones that hurt?"

"Sorry Lotte. Please don't be mad."

Lotte felt Allegra's genuine distress as the child stood rigid before her, lips quivering and eyes wishing for forgiveness. Gone was the willful, little, rather-do-it-myself girl. This one was full of anguish beyond anything merited by Lotte's mild disapproval. Was Allegra's concern for saying "dummy" because it was hurtful? Or, more likely, did she fear Lotte's rejection because of what she'd said? Lotte knelt and put her arms around Allegra's stiff little body.

"I forget sometimes," Allegra said in a meek, rare-ly-heard voice.

"Easy to do," comforted Lotte, "and I speak from experience. We all need to watch our words sometimes,

Honey Bun. Me too." Lotte hoped this was the right tack to take. "Here, wear this hat of mine you like so much. Later we'll get you one of your own just like it."

"No thanks," Allegra bounced back. "My hands are full of compost."

Rather than try to make sense of Allegra's logic, Lotte set the old, wide-brimmed straw hat on her own head and brushed a piece of lint from her jacket sleeve. She glanced into a nearby mirror, then blushed at her obvious vanity. *No need to primp for the garden,* she admonished silently. No need for primping ever again for that matter, and certainly not for that good-looking Mr. Adams, who she was sure they'd meet up with in the garden. She picked up the shovel in one hand and stuffed two pairs of garden gloves into the canvas bag with the other. *On second thought…*she looked in the mirror again, smiled, and tipped her hat fetchingly to one side.

Lotte locked the heavy door to the loft behind them. Allegra led the way, racing ahead to punch the down button on the old freight elevator. She laughed as the doors clanked open right away to her touch.

"Our lucky day." She grinned.

"Indeed it is, Miss Iris Blossom. Indeed it is."

MR. ADAMS

Mr. Adams was jamming a crushed Big Gulp cup he'd lifted from the sidewalk into a black plastic bag when he heard Allegra's greeting.

"We're here! We're here!"

He looked up from his work and watched Allegra and Lotte cross the street and enter the garden. The child ran to his side with Lotte following gracefully behind. *What a morning glory of a child,* he thought, as Allegra bent her head back to smile up at him. He bent himself forward to come closer to her size.

As Lotte neared, Mr. Adams stood up to greet her. *Now here's one beautiful lady,* he thought not for the first time about the handsome African-American woman standing before him in a rakishly tilted straw hat. How deeply she seemed connected to the earth, how her head seemed held high by the sky. He admired Lotte's gracious elegance, even when dressed as she was in gardening clothes—a faded purple T-shirt, well-worn blue jeans, and a silver-gray sweater that matched the color of her fashionably close-cropped hair. He gave Lotte only a mere nod, too shy to show the pleasure he felt in seeing her.

"Hey, look what I got for Godfrey," demanded Allegra. She lifted the lid off the compost container and shut it quickly. "Yuck, it really stinks."

Mr. Adams felt Allegra's hand gently pull on the pocket of his old tweed jacket. He sought Lotte's eye for approval as Allegra urged, "He's hungry. Come on, let's feed him."

"The whirlwind has arrived! She does have a way of helping you decide what you will do next, doesn't she?" Lotte laughed.

He felt Lotte's fingers brush his briefly as she reached for the bag in his hand. Though he checked, he saw nothing in her face to indicate her touch was anything but an accident.

"Here. Let me take up where you left off, Mr. Adams," she offered. "You have so much to do."

Too self-conscious to meet Lotte's eyes, Mr. Adams surveyed the crinkled candy wrappers, the old supermarket fliers, and cigarette butts that covered the lot around them. He wasn't sure he wanted to leave all that trash to Lotte. In fact, he would have happily spent the day cleaning the entire block with Lotte by his side. Yet this, he knew, was an admission he was too bashful to express aloud. Watching Allegra run toward the worm box, he decided to follow her lead, thinking it not too painful a choice at that.

When he reached the back of the garden, Mr. Adams could see Allegra had the worm box already open. He was proud of his construction of the sturdy, two-foot, square wooden box. Three trays fit neatly, one on top of the other, inside. Once the lid was off, he could look down into three-inch-deep soil atop the screened bottom; the second and third trays were the same, and the lowest tray lay on solid ground. He had designed it so that each tray had rope handles on the outside, making it easy for even tiny Allegra to lift.

This was only the latest of his garden creations, gifts that Allegra and Lotte seemed to enjoy so much—which added to his own pleasure in making them. While preparing for the spring groundbreaking a month earlier, Mr. Adams had crafted a simple wooden arch in his makeshift shop in the garage attached to his house down the street. A couple of students from the high school where he worked helped carry the heavy arch to the lot, where they dug holes and poured a cement base to keep it steady.

"Every garden needs an entrance," he announced

at the opening event, chuckling since the garden had no fence and anyone could enter anywhere.

He appreciated that Molly Rengate, the clergy-woman from the corner church, added her blessing that day: "Let this welcoming arch be a symbol of hope for what is to come."

The sight of Lotte delicately picking up a broken beer bottle jarred Mr. Adams back to the present, and he took in all there was still to do. The lot had been empty for more than a decade after a wrecking ball brought down the remnants of an old warehouse, the object of arson many years before. Despite their efforts, the land still gave off an abandoned air.

Rubble from the broken foundation remained, requiring them to build raised beds filled with clean topsoil. The soil depth along the garden's borders was sufficient only for wildflowers. He intended to ask Allegra to help sow the wildflower seeds he'd carefully harvested from plants native to the lot: fennel, yarrow, California poppies, and amaranth. He smiled at the intense yellow bank of volunteer mustard flowers already making a determined show, and noted that dandelions had marched out in force, too. *A ways to go, but coming along perfectly*, he thought with pride.

"Ugh." Allegra's grunt brought Mr. Adams once more back to earth.

"Need help?" he offered.

"Nope. I got it. I gotta make sure Godfrey doesn't squirm out."

He peeked over her shoulder at the newspaper strips and rotting table scraps inside the worm box.

"Not to worry," he said. "You've created a worm heaven. The only reason for Godfrey to leave would be for company."

"He's lonely?" Allegra squatted closer, her nose almost touching the box.

Mr. Adams admired the way her young bones could tuck so easily into a pretzel-position. He reflected that now, in his fifties, it had been some time since his own lanky body could crouch comfortably. But despite his limp—the relic of a tragic and still too-often-remembered accident—he felt limber and strong, at least on the outside.

"I don't know, but if he doesn't get company soon, the compost will take over. This is a lot of garbage to ask one worm to digest."

He stooped to pick up a wooden paint stirrer and, recognizing shredded and half-eaten denim jeans and old coffee grounds as part of the box contents, pushed them aside in his search.

"See him?"

"Not yet," answered Mr. Adams, handing the stirrer to Allegra. "Take this and see if you can find him. Godfrey may be so full from lunch he's hiding out. Is he napping in a corner?"

Mr. Adams sat down on an upturned, five-gallon, plastic paint bucket to watch. He'd scattered similar buckets around the garden as resting places for gardeners to enjoy a break or simply to watch others work. He was pleased to see that one of his makeshift stools was being well used by Mrs. Hatfield, a talkative elderly woman often joined by her children, grandchildren, nieces, and nephews. He recalled her saying she was Mexican, though her married name suggested other roots. Weakened by arthritis, she used a cane to walk two blocks from her home. She once told him she was grateful for a place to sit in the garden. She could regularly be found, as she was that day, amidst a little clutch of these "seats," an open invitation signaling she brought along a home-baked something to sweeten the gathering that flocked around her.

He noticed Mrs. Hatfield motioning for Lotte to join her on a nearby bucket. Lotte waved back as she tacked a new poem to the stand he'd built for her in the middle of the garden. "A community poetry board" she had called it, welcoming others to contribute. Mr. Adams reminded himself to read Lotte's latest poem before he left the garden. How enjoyable it would be to hear her read the poem aloud to him. He blushed at the idea, embarrassed at how often she showed up in his mind when he least expected her.

"Here, Godfrey. Come and get it. Nice fresh

garbage. Yummm." Allegra's sweet singsong inter-rupted Mr. Adams' train of thought. "Hey, there he is!" she exclaimed happily, her tone changing instantly to concern. "But he's not moving."

Grateful to turn to something he knew more about than women, Mr. Adams crossed one knee over the other and watched as Allegra poked the worm gently with her finger.

As he expected, she amended promptly, "Nope, he's okay." She lowered her face deep into the box and he heard her mumble, "But maybe he's deaf?" She raised her gaze up to him and matter-of-factly explained, "Deaf's when someone can't hear. Did you know that, Mr. Adams?"

Mr. Adams nodded. "I'm certain Godfrey heard you. Though not as you or I hear. Worms don't have ears."

"How can Godfrey hear me, then?"

"Ah, well you might ask. He has no eyes, either," he answered, thoroughly amused. He loved Allegra's curiosity and how quickly she was able to learn. She was charming even in her darkest moods, something he'd certainly witnessed in the past weeks since she'd come to the garden with Lotte.

He didn't know the details, but from the little Lotte told him he knew that this one had been through rough times. Having to leave friends and school in New York while her mother was in an alcohol treatment center must have been hard. He watched Allegra take a cooperatively lethargic worm out of the box and cradle it in her palm, and thought how lucky Allegra was to have Lotte take her in.

"Poor Godfrey's got no eyes!" declared Allegra as she gently scrutinized the worm in her hand. "But he's got lips. I see them. Do worms talk?"

Mr. Adams considered her question. "Worms can't talk the way we do, but they can listen. They listen to and send vibrations. So, in a way, they do talk. By feeling a vibration, they get clues to what is happening around them."

"What's a vibration?"

"Good question." Mr. Adams told Allegra to put her lips together and they hummed a tuneless duet softly until he couldn't help giggling from the tickle on his lips. "Did you feel the buzz?"

"Hmmm. Tickles."

"That is a vibration," he explained. "All sounds are vibrations. We can hear some vibrations, like bees buzzing, kittens purring, streetcars rumbling by. But worms can hear the slightest vibration in the soil. They hear even tiny bacteria decomposing, I mean eating, leaves and such." Allegra tilted her head, and Mr. Adams answered her before the question came to her lips. "Bacteria are tiny creatures, smaller than our eyes can see without a microscope."

Allegra's enthusiasm was evident. "I know what a microscope is. We had one in my school. It made bugs into monsters. My hair looked like a rope!"

"Exactly. Bacteria are tiny garbage workers of the world. They're everywhere." Mr. Adams pointed to the worm box. "Right now, billions of bacteria are inside there, working alongside Godfrey to make the soil rich and healthy for our garden." How he enjoyed Allegra's look of rapt attention. "And if all of us, worms and bacteria, rain and sunshine, you, Lotte, and me, and the rest of us keep making good garden soil, we'll attract even more bacteria and more worms. That's what we hope for."

"You sure know a lot about worms, Mr. Adams."

Pleased by her assessment, Mr. Adams smiled. "So do you, now, Allegra. So do you."

Mr. Adams was about to suggest they join Lotte and Mrs. Hatfield when he recognized a young man waving at him from the street.

"Who's that?" asked Allegra.

"It's Robin, a former student." Mr. Adams waved back, beckoning him to come.

"Are you a teacher, Mr. Adams?"

"No. I'm a janitor. I fix things at O'Connor High around the corner. Maybe someday you and Lotte can visit me there. My office, as some people call it, is in the basement. Kids seem to like to hang out there. You'd like it, too."

Mr. Adams lingered over the agreeable image of Lotte and Allegra visiting with him while students filtered in between classes and after school hours, as they did every day. Over the years, his basement storeroom and shop had become an underground haven for students, especially the ones who didn't quite fit in with the popular school crowd above. They'd come, find space on the floor, worktable, or folding chairs, and talk—or "shoot the shit," as they said when they thought he was out of earshot. The school's teachers and principals often asked him to keep an eye out for a kid who was having trouble. The administration let him know their gratitude by providing a steady flow of things for Mr. Adams and the students to fix—a lamp which needed rewiring, a chair with a leg missing, a worn-out desk desperate for sanding and painting.

"Hey, Mr. Adams," called Robin as he approached.

Genuinely pleased, Mr. Adams shook hands and introduced him to Allegra, explaining that Robin had offered to help with the garden straight away when they bumped into each other the week before. "So glad you came, thanks."

"No problem," answered Robin. "There's a bunch of last year's basement gang around with nothing much to do. Bet they'd be up for it, too. After getting us through the worst of high school it's the least we can do, Mr. A. This your little girl?"

Blindsided by the question, Mr. Adams was shaken to the core as he thought *of his little girl.* He sucked in his breath to try to hold back the recurring flashback of the long-ago accident. Vivid scenes came to his mind fast: snow hard on the windshield, hands tight on the wheel, headlights fast at them from the wrong lane, Marjorie, his beloved wife, reaching back to Julia's car seat... He gritted his teeth and willed the onslaught of images to disappear, knowing all too well the reality of what followed if he couldn't get a grip—the smell of antiseptic walls, the hopelessness of rehab, lost lives and dreams, the utter loneliness.

"Nope. He's not my dad. My dad's dead." Allegra's blunt response rescued Mr. Adams from his excruciating, well-worn nightmare.

"Uh, sorry," stammered Robin.

Mr. Adams's eyes met Robin's worried look, but before he could think of an appropriate response Allegra jumped up and slammed the top of the worm box closed.

"It's okay. I didn't know him anyway," she replied airily. "I'm gonna show Lotte how Godfrey's got only a mouth."

Mr. Adams watched Allegra depart. He sighed, not sure how to deal with his own and, likely Robin's, lingering confusion about what had just happened. He opted simply to affirm Allegra's resilience.

"She's okay, Robin. Not to worry. That little one's strong and she has Lotte, her grandmother, to take care of her."

He turned their attention back to the garden and the work before them. "How about we get those beds ready for the compost delivery next week?" Mr. Adams led Robin to three rows of 4-by-12 rectangular plots that were staked out with string. His tool bag was near a stack of lumber. After passing a hammer to Robin so they could nail the corner of a wooden frame for the first raised bed, he heard a soft thud and Allegra's high-pitched cry behind him.

Lotte was already by Allegra's side when he reached them. "Stupid, stupid, dirty, stupid brick," Allegra announced as she rebuffed Lotte's attempt to wipe tears from her face.

Mr. Adams followed Allegra's accusing finger to a loose brick some feet away and surmised that she must have tripped on it. He noted she'd skinned her knee and the palms of her hands on the gritty ground.

Lotte cradled the prickly Allegra in her lap, soothing. "You're okay, Baby Lark-ling. We'll go straight back to the loft and clean up."

Mr. Adams knelt down by their side and took a neatly folded handkerchief out of his back pocket. He pressed it lightly on Allegra's knee and held it there with the flat of his palm. Through tears, Allegra smiled up at him.

"Your hand's hot. Feels good."

"Ah well, let's see if it did the trick." Mr. Adams delicately pulled back the handkerchief and was relieved to see the bleeding had stopped. "Let's look at your palms, too."

As he reached for her hand Allegra jerked away and struggled to get up from Lotte's lap.

"Uh-oh! Where's Godfrey?" she cried. "Please, please, please Godfrey, don't be hurt."

"Oh dear. The worm," cried Lotte, raising herself from the ground. "Heaven help me, don't let that worm be underneath me."

Mr. Adams bent close over the brick where Allegra had fallen and widened his focus to reach a couple feet away in different directions. Robin and Mrs. Hatfield joined in the search.

Minutes later, Robin and Allegra exclaimed simultaneously, "Found him!" Each held a dangling worm between their fingers.

Mr. Adams realized they were 100 percent richer in worms. He grinned at Allegra as she, too, seemed to grasp the situation. Lotte stood and put her hands on her hips, laughing in that way of hers that Mr. Adams felt all the way to his toes.

"Look," called out Allegra, holding the worm between her fingers for Mrs. Hatfield to see. "Another worm. I fell on a brick and found another worm. Godfrey's got a friend."

Mr. Adams smiled as he saw Mrs. Hatfield, leaning on her cane, peer closely through her thick, dark-tinted glasses at the worm hanging from Allegra's fingers.

"Dios mio. Guapo, a real beauty."

"Uh-oh," said Allegra, "They need both his and her names."

Mr. Adams noted that Allegra seemed to have forgotten entirely about her fall and skinned knee. He smiled as Allegra repeated authoritatively to Lotte and Mrs. Hatfield the lesson he'd provided her earlier in the week.

"Worms need a girl's name and a boy's name, 'cause they're both boys and girls at the same time. They're...um, what's they called, Mr. Adams?" Before he could help her, Allegra already had the answer. "Don't tell, don't tell—Him...ma...fro...deets."

Mr. Adams didn't correct her pronunciation and suggested, "Ah, how about one of them can be Wilhelmina and Willie, after Queen Wilhelmina of Holland? Where my family came from."

"You lived in Holland?" asked Allegra. "Wow. Like Hans Brinker? Lotte read me the story, you know about the little boy who stuck his finger in the dike and saved everyone?"

Mr. Adams laughed, pointing south to a hill topped by the three-legged radio station antenna,

Sutro Tower. "No, actually. I grew up right here in San Francisco, high above the ocean, near the top of that hillside up there."

To himself, he mused, *she isn't so far from the truth.* It did often feel as though something had come unshored these recent weeks. He wondered what would happen when whatever lay behind his thoughts broke free.

NINA

"Get real, Nina. Yes, it's 2000. Okay, so it's a brand-new century, but good, old, time-honored greed's still got the upper-hand. We survived Y2K, but the name of the game is still dog eat dog. It's all about making a buck. 'What's fair' be damned. It's simply the way business is done."

Nina smarted at Marty's harshness and wished he'd temper his tirade—if not for her sake, at least so their son Raul didn't get the impression that it was okay with Marty that there was no difference between business and greed. There was no stopping him, though. Marty was on a roll.

"How that rubble patch you guys call a garden escaped notice until now is anybody's guess. No more, I'm telling you. Not after the TV coverage of your garden opening. Those cute kids running around?

The handmade arch? City politicos every-which-way-and-Sunday lining up for photo-ops? Wise up, Nina or hearts will break when they discover dreams don't always come true in real life."

Marty—her ex, a corporate real estate lawyer, and Raul's father—was Nina's best friend. *He has a point,* she conceded silently...*at least about getting on the ball to protect the garden.*

Aloud she retorted, "Yeah, yeah, yeah. I get it. I get it. Believe me, I get it."

The whole issue made Nina feel weary and grumpy. Once they'd finished clearing the supper dishes and said their goodnights, she followed Raul out the front door. Down Marty's steps she stomped, and then up her own steps into her house, next door. *But it's not like there's an extra minute to spare in a day,* she fumed to herself.

As the single mother of a teenager and the city's newly appointed Deputy Public Defender, time was something she didn't have to spare. Besides, who could guess what it would take to secure the garden's future? A mess of trouble, that much she knew. All it would take would be one greedy bastard developer making some sweet deal with one of the slimy members of the Board of Supervisors, and the bulldozers would be there before the first dandelion could be picked.

"Mom?" asked Raul cutting into Nina's internal

fulminations. "When are you going to stop calling Dad's girlfriend, 'Amy the Audiologist?' It's gettin' old. Time for you to move on, huh? I have. Cut her some slack, is all I'm saying. She's okay, and she totally gets it about you and Dad."

"And what exactly do you mean by 'totally gets it about me and Dad?'"

"Okay, I can see this isn't going anywhere. Forget it. I've got homework to do. Don't want to leave it. Tomorrow's jammed."

"Young man, homework can wait five minutes. Explain yourself, right now." Nina watched her son lean on the staircase banister heading to their second floor. *How tall he is*, she thought, amazed not for the first time.

"Okay. It's not like you need to be jealous or anything. Amy's not an idiot. She gets it, and it's okay. Hey. We live next door. You're in and out of Dad's place like it's ours. It *is* ours, in the modern-family kind of way you two have worked out. All I'm saying is it works out for all of us."

"What exactly 'works out?'"

"Okay, so you and Dad get to argue about who's right about how to change the world into a better place. You think the bad guys are the same ones Dad gets paid to defend, and he thinks you're an idealist with her head in the clouds who'd empty the prisons if you could. He likes to stash away money and you'd as soon give it all away. Me? I get the best of both worldviews, right? Kind of like growing up in the Glasnost years. That's what I mean by 'it works.'

"It's cool. For you too, yeah? You get to date who you like, as far as I can tell. Not that any of them stick around long enough even for supper. Look. All I'm saying is, Amy's cool. You should cut her some slack."

"Glasnost? When'd you get so smart?" Nina met Raul's grin with one of her own. Her rhetorical question might have seemed like circumvention to anyone else listening, but she recognized by her son's swagger—so much like his father's, when he knew he'd won—that Raul understood his point was taken. "Only thing...please stop with the gloating, will you?" She laughed.

Raul's observation was right on the mark. For the past half-year, Marty's girlfriend Amy was at their dinner table more often than not, and she held her own. Unlike any of Marty's other dates, Amy seemed fine with her boyfriend having a best friend who wasn't her. Nina resolved to do better.

"*Hijo.* Upstairs," she ordered. "Homework. Now. And yes, I will try about the Amy thing, I promise."

"'The Amy thing?'" Raul rolled his eyes.

"Get upstairs, kid," barked Nina in mock severity. Raul's laughter echoed down the staircase. She thanked her lucky stars that her son was showing every sign of taking on his father's good qualities—honest, smart, funny, loyal, and above all, kind. So different from the bad boys Nina seemed destined to pick for boyfriends. Why she couldn't go for nice men she couldn't (or wasn't willing to) figure out. Sighing, Nina left the question unanswered. She kicked off her imported JuJu Babe jelly platform heels and plunked her heavy leather Coach briefcase beside her on the plush living room couch. She settled into a well-worn nest of brightly colored throw pillows and reached around to snap on the reading light above her.

Instead of her client's file, she took a blank legal pad out of her briefcase and propped it on her knees. A scrawling, handwritten list of to-dos grew quickly down the page.

Marty's office:
A. *Title search—plat/lot, current owner, back taxes, liens, etc.*
B. *Appraisal lot survey*
C. *Battle strategy*

   …

Nina chewed the eraser end of her pencil. Marty would balk, of course. But she knew he would wrangle his office to come through, *pro bono*. She and Marty had had each other's back since Con Law class where they met at Stanford. The only two Latinos in their class, it felt only natural they'd gravitate toward each other. But like matching magnetic poles repel, their friendship took the form of disagreeing about everything. Everything, that is, except law. They shared a passionate belief that, through fair and systematic application of laws and regulations, the world would at least mitigate the cruelty and chaos of exploitation, poverty, greedy special interests, drugs, guns, and messed-up families.

Each earned full scholarships and understood the stakes. By working together, they found they worked better. They debated every point, of course, which proved a successful (if infuriating) strategy for learning even the most picayune details. After graduating in the top five of their class, they had their pick of jobs. It was no surprise when Marty signed on with McNamara and Fielding, San Francisco's most prestigious corporate real estate firm, and when Nina shouldered the PD's unending backlog of cases of needy, desperate defendants. That each was the first Latino lawyer in either workplace might have felt daunting and lonely, but they continued to support one another by meeting up most evenings after work to hash through their day and advise each other on the best ways to win their respective cases.

Raul's birth was a rocky time, no doubt about it. The pregnancy was unintended, the result of an especially late night together when a comforting snuggle led to the inevitable. Why they didn't marry made no sense to their parents or friends, but Nina and Marty knew if they married, they'd lose their best friend—or worse, end up killing one another…if not in body, then spirit. Marty came up with an ideal living arrangement when two little bungalows on Peace Street went on the market at the same time. His house had long been paid off in full. Hers? She figured maybe 14 more years still left on the mortgage. In any case, as Raul had observed only moments before, it all seemed to work out for the three of them.

Nina found herself warming to the task as her list continued to grow. She relished a good fight for a good cause.

Who?

Gardeners: Lotte, Mr. A., Mrs. Hatfield, Henry?

Supervisor Nunez?

SF Redevelopment?

Tax sale?

3. IRS 501-c-3?

4. Funders: Private, public, foundations?

Protecting the garden from development pressures meant everyone stepping up to the plate and doing the right thing. Lotte and Mr. Adams had to be brought on board, ASAP. Nina chortled as she pictured the gardeners storming the San Francisco Redevelopment Agency hearing room—Mrs. Hatfield's brood handing out chocolate-chip cookies while Henry pounded a table, holding forth about safeguarding artistic freedom in a democracy, and Mr. Adams mumbled politely in great detail about the best cover crops for soil remediation.

"Bring it on!" she whispered, feeling happy, even while knowing they had no reason to believe they'd succeed.

Nina yawned, put aside the legal pad, and settled in for a few more late hours with the thick client file beside her. Better get some traction on Monday's deposition before the weekend's distractions replaced any possibility for clarity.

LIZ

iz hated Sundays. For as long as she could remember, Sundays brought a kind of gloom that only intensified as the day stretched on. By evening she was often verging on panic. This Sunday, the gloom deepened with the reality of her circumstance.

Three weeks in and three to go. Liz shuddered, her chest tightening with the thought. Only the grit-hard promise of getting sober for Allegra kept her going.

"Watch out," she said testily, pressing into the sterile green wall of the rehab unit, barely avoiding a woman's elbow.

The woman, with her stringy blond hair, was clearly out of it. For the previous half-hour, Liz had fixated on her pace nonstop up and down the hallway, obsessively picking at the disheveled, green, cotton hospital "scrubs" that patients wore in their first weeks. The woman was driving Liz nuts and she vowed to trip her the next time she passed. But then the woman sat down and began to keen, as if in mourning, and Liz loathed herself for thinking meanly of someone so pathetic.

"Remind you of anyone?"

Liz turned to find Brenda, a rehabbed cocaine addict and now her treatment counselor, smiling at her. She'd grown fond of Brenda and had leaned hard into her at times. One moment she could be the kindly housemother, and later come at her with the ferocity of a tiger. This approach turned out to be good for Liz. For the first time, she had to face up to the limitations of her own wits and willpower, and she hated it.

"Get lost," joked Liz. She playfully eyed Brenda's baseball cap. "You know the Yankees are going to lose tonight, don't you?"

"It's all win-win to me," Brenda bantered back, tipping the cap's bill. Then Liz watched Brenda's face soften. "All set for your call home tonight?"

"Not really. I'm dying to hear Allegra's voice, and dreading it too. Can I reschedule to Monday? Sundays aren't good for me."

"Sorry, m'dear. You're stuck with Sunday. What's the big deal about Sunday? Want to talk about it?"

Liz sighed, knowing Brenda would pry it out of her

in any case. Growing up, she liked school for the most part, so anxiety about Monday's schedule wasn't the problem. More likely, it was the absence of any plan on Sundays and the weight of loneliness. As an only child with her mom barely remembered, Liz mostly fended for herself—especially on weekends. When her father, Vince, didn't have a visiting girlfriend there, he disappeared into his study for hours to nurse a succession of drinks while grading student papers. When he had a new love interest, he and his date stayed in the bedroom "playing Scrabble," or so he told her. As if she believed him. Liz tiptoed around the house, dreading more the politeness required of her when strangers were around than the loneliness and boredom of her solitude.

The greater part of the time, it was just the two of them—Liz and her father, rambling around the old, midwestern house with the wide front porch, watching the seasons change on the broad, tree-lined street. Liz had only the faintest memory of her mother, and she suspected these memories were made up of wishes.

Once Lotte came to live with them, things changed. Lotte was up early even on Sundays, bustling about with something to do. She'd make a pancake breakfast to lure Liz into conversation, or make some other obvious attempt to fold the three of them into the semblance of a family. By then, Liz was a teenager ready to repulse the slightest attempt at connection.

"And exactly when did you grow out of all that bristling-at-connection business?" asked Brenda, smiling. "Do tell."

"Give me a break, will you?"

Liz recognized that she was being teased, but it still bothered her that her most private thoughts were fair game. From the time she checked herself into the treatment center it felt like staff had never been off her back. The boot camp regimen rubbed hard against her sense of freedom, but it was also strangely comforting in one sense: no decisions needed.

Even the weekly calls home were scheduled and time-limited: an hour on the phone at most, though she never stayed the full hour. As much as she ached to hear Allegra's voice, the pain was sharper when she finally did, reminding her of the distance between them.

"Recovery takes all your courage and then some," said Brenda, interrupting Liz's thoughts. "No need to do it alone. Connections open the heart, remember that."

"*Right*," said Liz sarcastically, drawing the word into two syllables. "And an open heart is good for exactly what?"

Overcome by sudden nausea, Liz didn't wait for Brenda's answer. She ran for the bathroom, where dry heaves left her breathless and exhausted. Only the cool edge of the toilet bowl brought some relief. Then, kneeling on the cold tiles of the bathroom floor, she was no longer alone. She felt a cool washcloth on her brow and heard Brenda's soothing voice.

"This is gonna pass, Liz. I promise. Bear with me a while longer. You will feel better."

If anything convinced Liz never to drink or use drugs again, it was the prospect of repeating the hell of these past weeks of withdrawal. She swore, *never again,* and prayed Brenda was right and that the agony would subside.

"Why don't you tell me about Jonathan, Allegra's father?"

Incredulous, Liz lifted her head from the toilet bowl and swallowed hard. "Now? Here?"

"Can't think of a better place," answered Brenda. "It's private here, and clean. A little unorthodox, perhaps, but not uncomfortable. I brought in a pillow to cushion my butt so I can lean my back against the wall here, see?"

"You're insane."

"You may be right. But hey, why not? Got nowhere else to go, do you? No time like the present." Brenda held up a bottle of water. "Here, take a sip to wash out the nasties. I brought a blanket too. Twist around and put this on you. You'll feel better."

Shivering uncontrollably, Liz felt ridiculously needy. Yet she could see Brenda planned to sit her out. She wrapped herself in the blanket and focused on a barely visible spot on the linoleum floor in front of her, much as a ballet dancer might to steady herself while twirling on one foot. It seemed to help, and so did Brenda's encouraging patience—as palpable as an embrace. Time stopped. Her words flowed without stop.

"In high school, I was sort of a prude about drugs, and the boozers were slobs. But I drank some to keep my dad company. It was only a problem after Jonathan left me, but not when we first met."

Liz's story described the day she met Jonathan in her early student days at UC Berkeley. "I loved Cal. It was like I'd come home to my own after an accidental birth in a Nowheresville midwestern hospital. I loved the professors, and the homework was easy for me."

She explained how when Lotte moved in, their dinner table transformed into a give and take every night that was great preparation for her college courses. Lotte insisted Liz join them for what she called a "sit-down meal" of food and talk. They discussed current events, human nature, town politics, race relations.

"I was expected—no...*required* to hold my own. I hated it at the time, but it made speaking up in college classes seem like a piece of cake. After class one day, I felt this tap on my shoulder." Liz relished the unexpected memory of sweetness from that touch, like the smell of honeysuckle in late June. "I can still feel it now; it seems so real. This handsome guy—an African American upperclassman is standing there, wearing an Oakland A's cap, a hooded CAL sweatshirt, shorts, and Birkenstocks. He's a head taller and I had to look up to see his face. He is grinning..."

Liz paused and held her breath. How could she talk about their love? She'd forced herself to forget every bit and tucked everything deep inside. It was too tender, and way too sad.

"Breathe. It will help," whispered Brenda. "You're doing great. I'm right here."

Liz let out her breath. "Okay. We were in love. Sounds corny, but we were. Being together was the only place we wanted to be."

She told Brenda about the evening they took a bus from campus to Lake Merritt in Oakland. They walked the shoreline to a tiny floating dock used for launching rowboats during the day, and turned it into a dance floor that night. She taught Jonathan to waltz, one-two-three. He taught her the Harlem shake. Commuters honked and waved from their cars as they whizzed by.

"It was crazy...crazy love, from our first and every after step. He took me to jazz clubs where writers and poets slapped palms and called each other 'Bro.' Late at night in the dorm, he played guitar and taught me the blues. His 'Motherless Child,' he called me. We sang that old song again and again. It was the first time I knew I was a singer." Liz's voice softened to a whisper. "No one's held me like that since... Things went bad in the fall semester of my junior year."

Steeling herself, she hastened through the chronology of the collapse. Once Jonathan graduated that spring, he was accepted into Berkeley's grad program and they planned to move into an apartment together.

"But by mid-summer—idiot that I am, I flew out to Kansas to be with Dad, who called and said he needed me." Liz sighed and explained that Lotte broke up with Vince that year and moved back to San Francisco, because she learned he was sleeping with one of his students. "I was so disgusted with him. That he'd fall for one of his students and leave Lotte, who was like a mother to me. For God's sake—the girl was a year younger than me. Of course, it didn't last—they never did. When the girl left for a boy her own age, Dad went berserk. Stupid me, when he called, I thought maybe I could help. Wouldn't you know, though? When I got there, he was back to his old, depressed self. Bottle in hand, he disappeared into his office, and we spoke only in passing the whole time."

"That must have been hard for you."

"I guess. I was pretty down when I got back to Berkeley, but it all got a lot worse, fast."

Liz explained that the minute Jonathan met her off the plane in Oakland, she knew something was up. It turned out he'd taken a full fellowship at Middlebury's prestigious international relations PhD program, and was heading for Vermont in two weeks.

"I was devastated, then furious. When I demanded he turn them down, he said it was a fait accompli. I begged, 'What about our plans? What about Berkeley's grad program? What about me?'"

Liz scoffed at Jonathan's insistent promise to stay true, long-distance. How could she trust him? They were separated for only a few weeks, and he'd forgotten her completely. He ruined their future without thinking for a minute of what she might want.

After that, "Vodka was my regular companion. I spent the next few months drunk...until I learned I was pregnant. Jonathan came back for one horrible visit earlier that semester, and I blew it."

Liz hadn't take care—only that one time. The seed was planted, and a new life had begun.

Liz balled her fists to stop the tears, cursing herself for what felt like the ten thousandth time for that single mistake. How could she have been so stupid? Thinking back, she wondered, was it actually a mistake? Or was it pathetic self-deception that made her grasp at this one last straw? Had she really believed having a baby would bring them together again?

She felt Brenda incline closer toward her and recognized it as subtle encouragement for her to continue. At first, she explained, Jonathan seemed happy about the pregnancy when she told him on the phone. Soon, however, he began coming up with excuses—about why the time wasn't right for her to visit, or why another trip west wasn't possible for one reason or another. Often, he didn't pick up when she called for their regular phone dates, simply saying later that he forgot. When they did speak, their conversations ended in arguments—either with her accusations that he wasn't there for her, or his anger at her slurred speech and accusations of her drinking too much.

Eyes locked on the floor, Liz described the night she last saw Jonathan. He had flown into town, unexpectedly. "He was bawling like a baby, and told me some bullshit like, 'Things are too heavy. I can't do this father thing. My whole life's ahead of me.'

"When he said he'd go with me for an abortion, I grabbed a bowl from the table and threw it at him. I missed and it broke into pieces against the wall. I screamed, 'What about me?' Did he think I was ready for 'the mother thing?' Shit! He didn't stick around to hear the rest."

She recalled in excruciating detail how Jonathan put on his jacket and zipped it closed. She shouted at him, "Oh no you don't, you bastard. I'll show you."

She kicked him out before he could walk out on her and the baby growing in her womb. She grabbed his arm and pushed him toward the front door, heard him stumble and slam the door behind him.

Liz looked into Brenda's open face. "Really, it was only then that I realized what I'd done. From then on, I was on my own, alone."

Her nausea returned. She wiped her face with her sleeve. Her stomach cramping, she rushed through the remainder of the story. Despite the humiliation, she left Jonathan phone messages unanswered and threw out his unopened letters. She heard through the grapevine he'd found someone else. Of course. In a way, it was a relief. It made it easy to cut him cold out of her life. He was dead to her and the coming child, forever.

She dropped out of college without leaving a new address or forwarding information. She moved in with Lotte until Allegra was born, and—remarkably—stopped drinking. Waiting tables at a grungy San Francisco bar was the one job she found available without a BA. The bar had an open mic stage where staff and sometimes strangers off the street performed for free. One night, her boss heard her humming in the kitchen and told her, "Hey, you've got a pretty good voice." He encouraged her to try out in front of an audience.

Where she found the courage to sing on stage, she didn't know. But to her amazement, from that night on and over the next two years, she built a fanbase of sorts at the bar and started singing at other small-time gigs. Lotte gifted her with singing lessons with one of her friends, Winn. He taught Liz to sight-read, a better way to breathe, and how to get the most out of what had been her untrained voice. Pretty soon, she had a respectable repertoire of jazzy pop tunes, favoring a bunch of Ella's blues.

Brenda asked if this was when her drinking got out of control.

Liz nodded. "After Allegra was born, there was no need to hold back, and I had a new excuse to start drinking again. Vodka tonics worked wonders to loosen my vocal chords.

"Things were okay for a while," she continued. "A drink before singing to give me the courage to start and one after to celebrate success. The serious drinking didn't start till I moved to New York."

Liz forced herself back to fogged-over memories of that time—how she was 'discovered' by some guy with so-called connections back east, and how she took the bait. She and Allegra moved to the Big Apple, where she found a nanny for Allegra so she'd be free for the Big Time. Once there, she discovered competition was fierce—and what gigs she lucked on disappeared when the economy tanked. Stress was the reason she gave herself for drinking pretty much all the time. "It got harder to get up the nerve to sing, and my voice showed the strain. Lyrics slipped away in the middle, then beginnings of a song, and finally, even the closing words disappeared altogether. I went flat on the high notes. More vodka helped, or so I thought."

Yet more and more booze helped less and less. Worse was Allegra tiptoeing around the house. Gone were her adorable antics. "One morning, she brought me aspirin and orange juice in bed, can you believe it? She looked so sad. 'For your headache, Mommy,' she said.

"I was stealing Allegra's childhood and hurting the person I loved most in the world. Didn't stop me, though. Each morning began with resolve. By ten o'clock though, I was slumped in front of the TV, tumbler in hand and a bottle on the table. I didn't move till Allegra returned from school.

"One night, I was booed off stage. I'd slurred through what I remembered of the song I was singing." What little pride remained was gone. "The rest is history, as they say. Here I am. A drunk." Liz closed her eyes and sighed.

"What are you feeling right now?" asked Brenda.

"Right now? Nothing. Nothing at all. Except I'm gonna be sick again if you don't get off my back."

Brenda's next words sounded jumbled and far-off, as if coming from the hallway. "The nausea, the numbness, the anger. They're deflecting pain. Pain from a series of uncontrollable and very sad events that happened in your life. If you don't go in there and clear out the memories, you will drink again. I promise."

"No, I'm not...I'm not," Liz insisted. "Never, ever."

"Only three weeks left here, Liz. We're all going to do our best. I know you will, so you don't leave here without going into and through your pain. I'll be here with you and everyone else will, too. We've all been to the same god-awful place you find yourself in now. There's a better place opening for you, I promise."

Liz shook her head. She felt more defeated than ever. How could torture be helpful?

"I suggest you shower now," continued Brenda. "Change out of those scrubs into your own clothes. You earned them tonight. You did great, Liz. Walk outside before your phone call and breathe some fresh air. A new life is waiting."

"Shit, the phone call." Liz's nausea returned.

"There's love waiting on that line, Liz. You'll be fine."

Liz stepped into the airless booth and dialed her long-distance access number, then Lotte's phone. On the first ring, she heard Allegra's voice. "Mommy?"

"Oh Allegra. How are you, sweetie?" Liz asked, gripping the phone with one hand to her ear and twining the phone cord in her other. She hoped Allegra didn't pick up on the internal mess she was experiencing.

"I'm fine, but how about you, Mommy?" Liz heard the familiar sound of urgent worry in Allegra's tone.

"I'm doing better, really. Especially when I hear your voice. I miss you so much."

"Me too, you."

"Tell me everything about what's going on. How's your garden growing?" Liz hoped that the subject would take Allegra's attention elsewhere.

Bingo. Allegra was off and running about the comings and goings of the garden. Liz's body relaxed as she listened to Allegra list all the seeds she had planted. "You can't see anything yet. But Lotte says they're busy growing underground."

It confused Liz when Allegra got onto something about worms being boys and girls and how they needed two names. But she didn't even try to get it straight. Allegra sounded happy and free, and into this garden and her new friends. When Liz's tears came and her whispered sob broke through, she knew they were happy and sad tears together.

Allegra interrupted, "Don't cry, Mommy, Godfrey doesn't mind being called Godfrieda sometimes, honest."

Liz laughed, silently thanking God or who or whatever for her child's bizarre sense of humor. "Oh yes, I'm sure he—I mean, she—likes having two names."

"Mom, do you think I should have another name too?"

Wondering what this could be leading to, Liz tried to match Allegra's seriousness. "Why would you want another name? Allegra is such a pretty name."

"Uh-huh, but Mr. Adams says there's a boy part in me too."

"He does? What do you think he means by that?"

"I don't know. I'll ask him," said Allegra.

Baffled at what to say to all of this, Liz merely asked Allegra to, "Please tell him hello for me, okay? He sounds like a nice man."

"Okay. I'm going with Lotte and Mr. Adams to visit a school. There's lots of kids there, and a garden, too." The line went silent for a moment. "Mom? Maybe I'll go to school here until you come back?"

Liz sensed the fear behind Allegra's question and rushed to reassure. "Sweetie pie, I'll be there in three weeks, I promise. That school sounds like fun. They'll be lucky to have you."

When Allegra didn't respond, Liz asked what else

was going on, hoping to keep their conversation going. But no.

"Here's Lotte."

Allegra's abrupt ending startled Liz. She barely got her ground again when Lotte's voice came on the line. "Liz? How are you feeling, child?"

"I'm doing okay, Lotte. Better. You'll see." Into the long pause that followed, a puzzled Liz asked, "Are you still there?"

"I am. Just waiting here to hear the truth, that's all."

"The stillness of a Buddhist waiting for truth." Liz laughed, reminded of the affection she felt for Lotte. "Sorry. Didn't know I was that revealing. You know it gives me the creeps to be heard so carefully. They do the same in the recovery group, only they're not so subtle."

"Like how?"

"Like when I told them how much I loved Jonathan, they questioned how real my feelings were," Liz blurted, surprising herself for being so forthcoming. "For a time, they made me question how committed I really was to him. Oh, Lotte!" She burst into unwelcome tears. "How could he have left me...us? Gone off so soon with someone else? It's pathetic, but I really loved him so much. Or at least I thought I did, anyway."

She explained that the day before, when somebody in the therapy group asked her, "Why didn't you fight for him if you loved him so much?" She couldn't answer. Maybe she was the one who walled herself off—not only from him, but from everyone. Using alcohol to make sure no one could get through.

Liz quickly switched gears. "But really, Lotte, how is Allegra?"

"Doing well. She's full of beans. A bundle of joy. Whatever else went on in this one's short life, she knows one thing—she knows she is loved by both of us."

Liz drank in Lotte's assurance, but hurriedly answered to suppress her rising guilt. "We can thank the grace of angels for that. Allegra was born happy, I think."

"We can thank you too, Liz. She had good mothering from you, right from the beginning." Before Liz could respond, Lotte added, "Now don't say anything, sugar, just let that sink in."

Liz did let the word "sugar" soothe a wounded place inside, and her mind drifted to a memory of the first real hug when she let Lotte in…

"You there?" asked Lotte, grabbing Liz's attention back to the phone in her hand.

"Uh-huh. My mind wanders these days. I'm sorry. Hard to focus. But yes, I'm here."

"Good. I want you to know three things. You already know Allegra loves you? Well, I need you to take in that I love you too."

"I know that. Thanks, Lotte. I love you too."

"And my heart's broader for it. Here's the third thing you also need to hear: Liz, your father loves you."

Liz's temper flared. "Yeah, *right*. Like I'm ever going to believe that? How'd you get him to pay for this, anyway?"

"Oh Liz, he's dying to help. He never knows how, but he's not a bad man and he loves you more than you can imagine."

"More than I can imagine? You are right, there," replied Liz, feeling her defenses harden.

"We all do the best we can, Liz. My sense is you're looking pretty hard at yourself these days, yes?"

"Uh-huh," Liz responded quickly to end the conversation and her angry thoughts. Lotte said nothing, and Liz admitted, "Okay. Sure. I have anger issues. I'm trying to deal with them and everything else, 'the best I can,' as you say."

"Sounds like you're taking care of yourself. Remember, this is your time, and rest assured all's well here."

"Listen, I'm really sorry, Lotte," Liz interjected. Hating her cowardice, Liz lied, "Someone's rapping on the door to use the phone. I've got to hang up."

Without saying goodbye or waiting to hear Lotte's reply, Liz placed the phone in the receiver and collapsed into a crumpled ball of tears on the floor of the booth.

SUMMER

Today, I walked past a garden between the cut of two
buildings and felt an overwhelming urge to indulge
in untrimmed hedges and folly in untouched soil.
Day by day I've walked passed but never actually had
time to realize how beautiful this garden was.
The shrubs that went untamed.
The plants festered with weeds.
Upon opening the gate I felt a sense of relief, without
need for gloves I toiled in the dirt.
Spending a countless number of hours cleaning the
trash against the fence,
Grabbing stakes of wood and string,
Reinforcing the plants that grew wildly.
A disposition that no one cared.
I saw a bit of myself in this garden,
Pricked by the bushels of thorns, I felt resistance in the
need to tidy up.
Figuring the time it would take tending to every plant,
repotting and replanting.
The moisture felt from the soil under the grit of my
nails.
The rustle of leaves whispering thank you beneath the
sound of the wind.
The more time I spent here, the more that desire grew,
flourishing back to life.
No longer deemed remissive, the sun shone against the
new growth of petals.

Kewayne Wadley. https://www.poemhunter.com/po-
em/community-garden-4/

LOTTE

otte swiveled in her desk chair to greet Liz tiptoeing through the front door of the loft. Nine-forty already? Time passed so quickly.

Since Liz's return from rehab, Lotte cherished the few quiet hours when Allegra was tucked in bed and Liz was away at AA meetings. She forced a smile and was pleased to see Liz grinning back. Liz was so changeable these days that Lotte didn't dare predict what mood she would bring in the door.

Lotte stood to put the kettle on and asked, "Want tea?"

"Hmmm, I think I'll have chamomile...or maybe some hot milk," answered Liz. "But let me do it, Lotte. You sit."

Lotte gave way to Liz and moved to the couch.

She watched Liz reach into the fridge, pull out a milk carton, and pour it into a pan.

"How about you?"

"Chamomile, thanks," answered Lotte, gladdened by the sound of Liz's soft humming as she busied herself in the kitchen. Lotte clapped when Liz set the tea mug on the table with a flourish and curtsied, exclaiming, "Voila!"

"It's good seeing you happy, Liz. What's up?"

"I got a job. Waitressing. My forte. Nick, a guy in AA—he's my sponsor, in fact—offered me work at his club. It's part time, but...I think it could turn into much more."

Lotte tried to hide her crestfallen feelings. On the one hand, she wanted to affirm Liz's enthusiasm, but on the other...it did raise a red flag of foreboding. Going from rehab to work anywhere near a bar or a club? How could this be good for someone newly sober and wanting to stay that way? Lotte's hand shook slightly, spilling tea on the table. She was well aware that her rapid clean-up response didn't mask her sense of unease, nor must her wrinkled brow appear to be a vote of confidence.

"Lotte, stop worrying so much," Liz sputtered defensively. "I am not going back to drinking. I promise. Yeah...I get it, that it's a bar. But I'm okay, really. I know I can handle it."

That answer was not reassuring. Neither was Liz's

explanation that half the barstaff belonged to AA, nor the fact that the bar-owner, this *Nick* somebody, was a 15-year AA member who planned to share the same work hours as Liz to offer his support. Lotte's suspicions were raised. Who was this guy, and what did he want from Liz? If she could, Lotte would wrap Liz in a protective cocoon to keep her safe from men like whoever this Nick fellow was. Knowing the futility, she shared none of this concern with Liz.

"One night a week, I'll get to sing," Liz told her. "At least, I hope so. I have an audition set up with Nick's piano guy who's coming on Wednesday. Can you and Allegra come and cheer me on?"

Lotte nodded, mulling over the insistent question of why, ever, a recovering alcoholic would want to serve people alcohol. To her, it made no sense.

"Please be happy for me. I'll be singing again. It's the one thing I was good at, and I really believe I can make a go of it again. Don't you want me to get some more mileage out of those singing lessons with Winn that you arranged when I was pregnant, back when you wanted me to move in here so badly? You said I had to, quote, 'sing for my supper.' Remember?"

Lotte smiled begrudgingly, choosing not to correct Liz that she was who had shown up on Lotte's doorstep. What emotional wrecks they'd both been. Liz called it their "Broken Hearts Hotel," each clutching her own Kleenex box and watching Liz's belly grow.

When Liz moved closer on the couch and laid her head on Lotte's shoulder, Lotte capitulated. It would be good for all of them if Liz were singing again. Winn, her longtime friend, said Liz had real talent. She might have made it in New York, until her drinking dashed that dream. Maybe this time, with AA friends and family support…?

"I do love having you and Allegra close," Lotte admitted.

These past months with them had been all right, even with the rough spots. Grandmothering was more fun than she'd imagined, and it felt good to be able to provide a safe harbor for both her girls. With Liz back from rehab to share in Allegra's care, Lotte was freer to return to work, spend time with friends and the garden, and attend the regular meditation classes that sustained her in so many important ways. Things were going well…as well as could be expected.

"I can't wait to bring home a paycheck. I really hate feeling so dependent," murmured Liz.

Lotte wondered whether this was the time to tell Liz about the sublet upstairs? She decided to plunge in. "By the way, Antoine called this evening. He's got a Fulbright for Florence—a yearlong fellowship starting in August. He and Marie will stop in Paris to visit family first, so they don't have much time to rent their loft. He hoped you might be interested, and I think it's a great idea."

"You've got to be kidding?" Liz's rhetorical question hit Lotte full force. "Where in hell do you think I am going to get that kind of money? You're so la-la land, Lotte. My salary and tips can't pay rent, never mind food or anything else."

Silenced by the vehemence of Liz's reaction, Lotte took a moment to orient. She inhaled deeply to help her focus on the best way to respond. "I did think about the cost, Liz. It can help you toward the independence you say you want. And…hmmm…Vince wants to help."

Wrong again, realized Lotte upon seeing the stunned look on Liz's face. She sighed and sat back on the couch to wait out Liz's latest attack on her father.

"You should know better than anyone. He doesn't care about me, you, or anybody but himself," Liz shouted. "Besides, it feels like another rejection from you, just when I was beginning to feel at home here. I thought you were okay with us being here."

Reeling from the unexpected accusation, Lotte found no words to respond. How could Liz feel rejected by this idea of moving one flight upstairs?

"It's humiliating enough he paid the twenty

thousand for rehab," Liz hissed. "Besides, the rent up there must be, what? Over fifteen hundred a month?"

Does this question show interest? Lotte dared to hope. Seizing the moment, she spoke quickly while she had the chance. "Antoine and Marie are fond of you, Liz, and they need someone who will take care of their things and the place while they're gone. Yes, it is a bit high—two thousand a month, but they'll take care of the utilities and aren't asking for last month's rent upfront. Very generous, I'd say..."

"You think Vince has this kind of money? You've got to be kidding," interrupted Liz.

"Ask him for three thousand so, along with your paycheck, you'll have some savings to help when they return and you and Allegra are on your own." She rushed on before Liz could object. "And yes, your father has money and can afford this. He may be a Marxist scholar, but that's only one of the contradictions he lives with. He didn't sock his salary under the bed all these years, Liz. His investments have done well. Nor did he spend it on all the young women he took under his wing." Lotte inhaled, momentarily derailed by annoyance with herself for this unnecessary dig, yet she barged forward. "Vince is a wealthy man." Lotte locked eyes with Liz to drive her last point home. "... and nothing would help heal his very, very tender heart more than to be able to help you and

Allegra—and me, for that matter—in any way he can. You need his help. And he needs to help."

Lotte watched Liz stand dramatically, turn, and walk to where her jacket hung. She pulled it on, flung her purse strap over her shoulder, and strode to the front door. Lotte dared not move a muscle for fear that Liz's anger would escalate. She did not want to be the origin of or witness to an explosion she knew might come if she spoke another word. Silently she pleaded, *Don't go out that door, Liz. Don't drink over this, please.*

"You and your goddamn pious Buddhism," shouted Liz. "You sit there and don't react. It's like you're made of stone. Can't you admit you want the place for you and your new boyfriend?"

Lotte flinched as Liz slammed the door.

Boyfriend? Where did that come from? Lotte drew a blank, then turned a deep burgundy recalling Allegra's similar intimation when Mr. Adams joined them for dinner earlier that evening.

It had been a spontaneous invitation, after a day in the garden getting the stage ready for the next day's gala performance—the garden's Fourth of July "Inter-dependence Day" celebration, which happily coincided with Allegra's sixth birthday.

After dinner, when Mr. Adams was ready to leave, the child looked at them and declared, "You two should get married."

Mr. Adams laughed and asked, "Why is that?"

Allegra easily responded, "So you can sleep over and you and me can have breakfast together here."

While embarrassed at the time, Lotte hadn't given the incident a second thought until now. *Boyfriend? Mr. Adams? First Allegra, now Liz? What are the girls picking up on that I'm missing?* She dismissed the idea and returned to her more serious concern...Liz, on the street, at night. *Will she be safe? Will she drink again?* Lotte sighed and picked the cups up from the table.

With little conviction, but hoping to bolster her resolve, she murmured aloud to no one, "There is nothing I can do or not do to stop Liz, if that's what she decides to do tonight. Nothing except...take care of myself."

The best way Lotte knew to do this was to gather herself together and sit on her meditation cushion. She checked on Allegra first. The child's breathing was deep and even. Good. Hopefully Allegra had slept through her mother's outburst. Closing the door gently, Lotte crossed the living room.

She bowed once then knelt on the cushion, pulled her legs around in front of her, yogi-style, and glanced at the clock. 10:26. Chilled, she reached for an earth-toned wool shawl folded beside her on the mat and pulled it around her shoulders. A vivid image of Liz stomping up the empty street, alone and forlorn, awash in anger and tears led Lotte to breathe out a mute prayer. *May you be safe and warm and find peace.*

Slowly, she drew in a breath and an image of John Adams replaced that of Liz. *He does have a kind face,* she admitted. *But absolutely no way.* She had no time for a man, and no white man, for sure. Not after the mess with Liz's father, Vince. Lotte caught herself and whispered aloud the word, "Thinking," using that label to silence her train of thought before it went any further. She exhaled and expected the usual serene sensation to follow, but before her next inhalation she heard Allegra's voice in front of her.

"Lotte?"

Lotte opened her eyes to find a sleepy Allegra clutching a well-worn stuffed dog against her flannel pajamas, her lips pursed.

"Pumpkin, come here." Lotte opened her arms and snuggled Allegra into her lap. "There you are, sugar. Everything's okay."

"No, it's not," came Allegra's muffled response.

Knowing Allegra would explain herself in her own time, Lotte patted the child's spongy cushion of delicate curls and waited.

"Did I make Mom angry again?"

Lotte looked into Allegra's upturned face, shiny now with tears. "No, darlin'. Your mom left so she could figure things out. She'll be home soon. You know how it is. Sometimes we need to be alone until hard feelings blow over." Lotte took Allegra's nod for understanding.

She started to explain that Liz's testiness was due to her new sobriety. But mid-sentence, Allegra sat up and put a gentle hand over Lotte's mouth.

"I don't wanna talk about it anymore."

"Okay. Want me to tuck you in and tell you a story so you can go back to sleep?"

"Yup. But can Mr. Adams sleep over soon?"

Lotte closed her eyes and inhaled slowly to hush the onslaught of her own raw feelings. *Enough of this*, she thought. *I'm not ready. I don't want Mr. Adams or anyone else in my bed*.

"Are you sleeping?"

"Just thinking," answered Lotte. "You like him, huh?"

"Yup. And he likes worms, dirt, wildflowers, and me."

"That he does, Twiddly-pop. What do you say we go to bed now for a little dreamtime?"

"And you know what, Lotte? He likes you, too."

"Uh-huh. We'll see, little one. We'll see.

LIZ

eeling better after her morning shower, Liz gulped her cold coffee and dressed hurriedly in a classic black shift and matching sandals. She threw a broad turquoise scarf over her shoulders and left the apartment. On the street, Liz adjusted her sunglasses to cut the mid-morning glare. Her eyes stung from a lack of sleep. Across the street, in the garden, she saw a dozen or more familiar faces setting up for Inter-dependence Day.

Back by the alley at the edge of the vacant lot was the gardeners' newly constructed stage, painted with a gaudy backdrop of huge flowers, bumblebees, and two handsome nudes discreetly draped with green-ery. Gold, satin sheets billowed over wobbly door frames and created stage-left and stage-right entrances, ready for the children's performance. Someone Liz didn't recognize was placing blankets on the straw bales intended as seats for the audience. Antoine and Marie, she noticed, were helping Mrs. Hatfield, who was fussing over the last decorating details of the refreshment table.

Refreshments…damn, Liz chastised herself silently. She'd fucked up, again, and left it all for everyone else to do. Not so much as lifted a finger to help Lotte with the oversized sheet cake she spotted on the kitchen table the night before…she, who used to love baking and decorating—was good at it, too. Liz slammed shut this stream of self-deprecation and instead took solace in mentally reciting one of Nick's personally altered AA mantras: "Stop kicking yourself. Others will do it for you if it really matters." After fleeing Lotte's loft in the night, she called Nick for help. Their conversation reinforced how talking it through with someone, not hiding behind a drink, was the best way she could take care of herself—and Allegra, too.

Intoning Nick's voice in her head, she felt almost ready to face the day. From the corner of her eye, she caught sight of Allegra running and laughing with a line of kids following her across the garden. Her heart caught in her throat to see her daughter so happy. And there was Lotte, beckoning her to join Mr. Adams and herself by the arch. Ashamed about her recent tantrum, she could hardly face herself, never mind face up to Lotte.

Nina's warm hug saved the moment and confirmed her tentative hope for a friendship with this feisty powerhouse of a woman. Their kids were friends. Allegra had an obvious crush on Nina's teenage son, Raul. Every chance she got, she dragged him to her sacred spot in the garden, the worm box. There, she regularly dangled worm after worm up to his face, introducing each by name. Once, when Liz mentioned to Nina how grateful she was for Raul's tolerance, Nina assured her, "Nonsense. He's crazy about her. She's the kid sister he's always bugging me for."

Amazed (and not a little intimidated) by Nina, Liz wondered how she held it all together and managed to look so great all the time. Even as a single mother and public defender working with hardcore murderers, robbers, and rapists, Nina seemed never to lose her cool. Liz wished she was as tough, smart, and funny as Nina, but then scolded herself to cut it out and met Nina's kisses on each cheek. Hadn't Nina, only two weeks earlier, told her that she was amazed by Liz? "Sing in public, are you kidding? No way," Nina had exclaimed.

"*¿Que pasa?*" asked Nina.

"Oh, you know. One day at a time," answered Liz, not wanting Nina to probe.

"Got that straight." Nina smiled as she linked Liz's arm in hers while they crossed the street. "Did Lotte tell you about the guy who came by the garden yesterday? He pulls up in his car, and watches us digging. We were mounding compost onto the beds. And he asks where the bodies are."

"Really? What happened?"

"Everybody got real quiet. Me, seeing Raul across the garden holding a shovel looking bored, I tell the guy, 'You know, it would definitely help my son's motivation to dig deeper if we found a human ear, or a thigh bone.'" Nina said her morbid joke apparently cut the tension, because, "Pretty soon the guy was out of his car hitting me up. But did he move an ounce of dirt? No way."

Liz was still laughing as they neared Lotte, whose arms were outstretched in welcome. *How can she put up with me?* wondered Liz, sensing no grudge in Lotte's full hug.

Liz shook hands with Mr. Adams, noting, to her pleasure, that he was looking particularly handsome in his long-legged corduroys and plaid flannel shirt. And was Lotte really wearing lipstick? Liz privately patted herself on her back. *At least I got something right last night. Something is definitely stirring between these two.*

"Look."

Liz turned to where Lotte was pointing and asked,

"Mr. Adams, what are the children doing over there in the wildflower patch?"

"Ah…" Liz's curiosity was piqued even more by Mr. Adams' hesitation. "I may be able to explain," he continued. "This morning, I showed Allegra a star mole tunnel and described how they eat worms like candy. You see, they paralyze their victims and carry them off to a holding tank, where they satisfy their appetites at leisure."

Nina expressed what Liz was thinking, "That's so, so horrible, Mr. Adams."

"'Gross,' was what Allegra called it," he replied, grinning. "She has a clear preference for the worms' side, as you might expect, and has mobilized a SWAT team of mole tunnel-stompers to drive off the moles. Ah…what more can I say?"

"So much for 'Inter-dependence' Day," remarked Lotte. "What about the poor mole? All his hard work laid flat?"

"Or *her* work?" Liz saw the twinkle in Mr. Adams's eyes as he teased Lotte, affirming her suspicions all the more.

Lotte crossed her arms, clearly feigning indignation before muttering, "Harrumph."

Enjoying their banter and the obvious affection growing between them, Liz wondered wordlessly how she got so lucky to have landed here with Lotte and these kind people. She found herself trying on the possibility that things might actually work out when Mrs. Hatfield's firm hug and compliment reinforced the feeling.

"Aren't you lookin' pretty this morning, chica?"

Liz mirrored the others' smiles as the elderly woman kissed first her, then Nina, Lotte, and Mr. Adams, each on both cheeks before recruiting Mr. Adams's help with moving the refreshment table with Antoine.

Shortly after they'd gone, Raul's father, Marty, and his girlfriend, Amy, came over. Marty said, "Don't look, but see that newbie over there? The one pretending to be helpful, spreading the blankets on the hay bales?" Marty turned his head slightly in the direction of the stage. "He's trouble, with a capital T. Check him out? Don't stare! See him? Now he's grabbing the table with Antoine?"

The man didn't look so bad to Liz. Buff, no doubt about it. Mid-30s, she guessed. Tan in a tanning salon kind of way, with thick, dark hair swept perfectly off his brow. She caught Nina's quick conspiratorial wink and knew sparks were about to fly between her and Marty, as usual.

Smiling broadly Nina quipped, "Yeah, right. Simply 'cause he's got a better tailor than you, Marty? Don't see a lot of suits like that in the garden, do we?"

"I mean it, Nina," Marty replied sharply. "Good thing we're getting on top of this mess, because that slick, overdressed, greedy son-of-a-bitch is here for one reason. He smells money. Horace Moon's his name, but he goes by Ace. AKA, the king of tax sales. He is one venal guy. A real shark. You guys better savvy up, or he will eat you alive."

"Moon, as in Antoinette Moon's son?" asked Lotte. "I know her from the Community Foundation. She's so lovely and very generous."

"Believe me, the lady can afford to be generous," replied Marty. "But mark my words, her son's beaucoup rich from a nice family, but he is not wired the same as his mother. The guy's a predator, I'm telling you. Where you guys see flowers and tomatoes all nice here in the garden…? Ace, he sees a high-rise. He'll be laughing all the way to the bank 'cause he'll pay peanuts for this lot if we can't stop him. Be careful today, got it? We got to keep lining up our ducks in a tidy row so we're ready when the time comes for a fight.

"But hey, that's not why I came over, Nina. Our son's pretending he's not got butterflies in his stomach, but truth is he needs a discreet Mommy hug before his band plays."

Alone with Lotte after they left, Liz picked up the concern in her eyes. She asked, "Do you think the garden will be okay?"

"Right now, it's not the garden I'm worried about, Liz."

Grasping Lotte's point, Liz rushed to reassure her. "I'm fine. Really." She raised her dark glasses to her forehead so Lotte could see her eyes. "I'm sorry for being so…oh, I don't know…awful. I don't know how you put up with me. I can't stand myself."

"It's true I was worried," answered Lotte. "I thought I heard you come in some time in the middle of the night, but when you weren't there this morning…"

"Oh God, I should have left a note. I'm really sorry," apologized Liz.

Of course, Lotte must have feared she was roaming the streets or worse, all night. She added "thoughtless" to her mental list of stop-kicking-yourself phrases.

"I got home after two. When I left, I walked around, banging my head against the proverbial wall, kicking myself for being such a bother to you and everybody. I really am sorry to have worried you. It took me time to know that what I really needed was to call an AA friend and get my head straight."

In the sleepless hours the night before, it became clear to Liz how much she and Allegra needed their own space, if for no other reason than to have the privacy to call her AA sponsor without freezing to death in a phone booth each time.

She told Lotte, "You're right. We really do need a place of our own. If you'll confirm with Dad for me…? I'm not up to it. Meanwhile, I'll talk to Antoine and Marie." She looked over at the newly positioned refreshment table and saw they were both still nearby.

Liz brushed her fingers through her hair and continued distractedly, "Where was I? Right. So I called Nick from the phone booth by the bus stop. Woke him up, but he said it was better I called than not. We met for breakfast and then went to a meeting together." Cringing, she tried to meet Lotte's eyes. "I know I should have left a note for you this morning. I'm such an idiot. I thought I'd be right back."

For no reason, Liz began to cry. She stomped her foot in frustration and turned her back to the garden crowd so no one would notice. She felt Lotte circle around her to keep eye contact. The situation abruptly struck Liz as so absurd she began laughing.

"Lotte, you are a saint," said Liz as she felt Lotte fold her into her arms.

Lotte whispered in her ear, "No, Liz. A saint, I am most definitely not. But I am here for you, as best I can. Always will be. We are family."

How sweet to burrow into this woman's generous shoulder forever, thought Liz. But instead, she lifted her head to explain, "Nick agreed with you, about what you said about Dad. He said it was pride keeping me from asking for help. Pride and…fear. Both are poison for an alcoholic, he said and…" The impact of Allegra's head hurtling into Liz's side stopped her words short.

"Mommy? You okay?"

Liz squatted down to Allegra's level. "I am, sweetie. Better 'n better, every day. Come here, Mommy needs a hug." She invited Allegra to move closer. Holding tight to her little girl, Liz said, "You are the best!"

Allegra asked brightly, "The best what?"

Liz laughed. "The best birthday girl ever born on the Fourth of July. That's who you are."

Allegra beamed, inhaled deeply, and opened her eyes wide. "Mom, guess what?" she asked.

Liz felt a light hand on her shoulder as Lotte indicated with a nod that she was going over to the stage. Liz turned to face Allegra who clearly had something important to tell her.

"What?"

"Mom. Josie's a man," whispered Allegra. To Liz, it sounded as if Allegra wasn't sure whether she had an inside scoop or if the information was too preposterous to be true.

"That's right," answered Liz, hoping to appear nonchalant.

"You knew?" a startled Allegra replied. Shaking her head as if in disapproval, she added, "but he…or she…I mean, she wears dresses, Mom."

"Pretty ones too, don't you think?" asked Liz.

A gay couple, Josie and Paulo, were key organizers of the garden. Liz liked them both. Paulo had been an actor with the National Conservatory Theater, a renowned repertory group. But his HIV progressed to AIDS, and crippled him with the multiple illnesses that came with it. He was thin as a garden post and unwell much of the time. He once told Liz that he took energy from being in the garden. Josie lovingly wheeled him there most every warm day.

The centerpiece of the Interdependence event was to be the performance Josie and Paulo scripted and rehearsed the previous week with the children. The kids helped make their own costumes and studied their lines together. Allegra learned hers by heart, practicing every night with Liz: "We are creatures of delight, from under the ground."

Fittingly, Allegra's dramatic debut was as a spokesperson for the earthworms, bugs, and other creepy crawly things from the underground. Liz noticed Allegra had not yet put on her costume but was wearing heavy mascara and rouge, no doubt thanks to Josie's artistic touch—and acquiescence to Allegra's insistent pleading.

"Mom!" Allegra wriggled free and stood with hands on her hips a little away from Liz. "How can a man wear a dress? Mr. Adams and Grandpa wear pants. Men are 'sposed to wear pants."

"Oh?" asked Liz with querying eyebrows lifted, pretending surprise. She slowly and deliberately looked down at Allegra's overalls and caught Allegra's eye briefly before turning to pointedly take in the sight of their neighbors. Most were wearing jeans or sweatpants. Mrs. Hatfield wore a sari, of all things. Henry had on a kilt. Liz recognized in Allegra's pout that she understood the soft spot in her logic.

"It's a little like Godfrey and Godfrieda, don't you think?"

Allegra rolled her eyes and heaved an exaggerated sigh. "Mom, Josie is not a worm."

"True, but check out the human beings around you. No one is the same. There's big people and little people and Black people like Josie and Latino people like Mrs. Hatfield, young people and old, even freckled people." Liz playfully touched the freckles on Allegra's nose, but Allegra shrugged her hand away. "...and people without freckles. And, people in dresses..."

"...and people who don't wear dresses," said Allegra, mimicking her mother's tone.

Liz cocked her head and changed the subject, "Nice makeup job, incidentally. You look ravishing."

Allegra batted her eyelashes, obviously pleased. She turned away from Liz then, announcing grandly in diva fashion, "Gotta go."

Liz's heart raced with pure love as she watched her daughter weave her way through the throng.

NINA

" i there," Nina said with a smile, trying to keep her voice innocent and friendly. "Can I help you?"

She was careful to avoid looking at Marty to see if he was watching her sidle up to Horace Moon. She knew Marty would be furious. In truth, she wasn't certain how or even if she should proceed. But when she glimpsed the pair of un-scuffed yellow-and-black, tiger-striped Nike Wu-tan Highs below the carefully tailor-sewn hem of his fancy slacks, she had her angle.

The man's got classy taste in shoes. Shoe vanity was something Nina knew about, firsthand. *Besides*, she mused as she barreled on, *what's there to lose?* As the saying goes, it pays to keep your enemies close.

Exaggerating her pose, Nina purposefully shifted her left foot in Ace's direction, showing off her own form of vanity—that day, a pair of four-inch Rocket Dog rainbow platform flip flops.

"Nice shoes," she observed casually, pointedly looking down at Ace's feet. "But don't let my son see them, or you might go home barefoot."

"Is that a threat or a compliment?" Ace sallied back, grinning.

Despite his smile, Nina knew from the subtle stiffening in his posture that she'd gotten Ace precisely where she wanted him: feeling a bit defensive. Her responding smile was genuine, though not for reasons he'd guess. *This bad boy was not only into expensive shoes,* strategized Nina, *he deflects his insecurity with a quick wit and an easy smile. This is going to be fun.*

"My name's Ace."

"Nina," she answered brightly, meeting his outstretched hand with a firm handshake and direct gaze into his pale blue eyes. "At your service. What brings you to the garden?"

"Nice day. Nice people. Heard things were happening for the Fourth and I thought I'd check it out. Impressive." He gestured broadly to take in the raised beds and the stage. "That cool with you? The party's not closed, is it?"

"Of course not," answered Nina. "Inter-dependence Day has no bounds. But you're a new face in the neighborhood, so people are curious."

"People? Or you?" Again, that broad grin.

He knows he's handsome, thought Nina. She flitted her lashes and bantered back, "Are you flirting with me?"

"Are you flirting with me?" he replied smoothly. Nina felt Ace bend in and arch over her ever so slightly. Attack or intimacy? She couldn't tell, but didn't wait to find out.

"Ha-ha. Funny guy, huh?" she answered, purposefully shifting toward him, close enough for him to pull back. She was a pro with the practiced, nonverbal subtleties of push-pull posturing. Tools of her trade when dealing with thugs or unwanted hugs, whether from clients, colleagues, or her legal adversaries. But nothing prepared her for Ace's next words.

"I guess you could say my family is from the neighborhood. We used to own the building that was here."

"Right. And the whole block used to be the upper left quadrant of my family's rancho," joked Nina. Immediately she regretted the historical misappropriation as Ace's eyes widened, clearly impressed. He obviously took her at her word.

"You go that far back?" he stated. "That is so cool!"

"Not exactly," Nina confessed. Her flippant comment had been intended to mock his story, but Ace's earnest response left her feeling caught out in a lie.

She winced mentally, knowing this would cost her the high road she was jockeying for. How many times had she admonished her clients that truth wins out every time over the loser's tactic of lying? "Only pulling your leg. My granddad came up from Oaxaca to work the docks."

"Oh well. That's cool too," replied Ace. Nina appreciated it when he followed with an admission of his own. "It wasn't our family's for long. My grandfather diversified after World War I. Sold most of the family's real estate before the Depression, including these two warehouses—the one that was here on this lot, and that building over there." Ace pointed to Lotte's building across the street. "They're architectural gems. Or were. Now, there's only the one left. Both buildings held up in the 1906 earthquake."

The guy's definitely comfortable holding forth on a subject, Nina observed. She followed his gaze as he raised his chin toward the garden's lot.

"Loma Prieta, our last big quake, damaged the building that was here beyond repair. After an arson fire, the city ordered it gone. They were both warehouses, of course. This whole section of town was chock-a-block full of warehouses, filling in here and there in a mishmash with residential houses and commercial storefronts. For a time, that beauty over there housed Whittier-Fuller's paints and pigments, until the company moved to Potrero Hill. Several soap manufacturers were here on this lot and before that a leather tanning operation used the building too, or so I remember.

"When warehousing moved to South San Francisco, both buildings eventually went empty, their windows boarded up. Gutted, of course. Anything metal, plumbing and what not, was long ago salvaged for scrap. Graffiti everywhere. So, when the demolition happened it probably was no big loss to anyone. The warehouse across the street remained an empty eyesore, like a forgotten beached whale, amid the debris surrounding it. It was refurbished with condos a few years ago. But you know all this, being in the neighborhood and all. Nice job they did with the condos. Whoever got in there when they did had foresight."

"That's so interesting," commented a dazzled Nina.

Despite better judgment, she found something beguiling about the depth and passion of Ace's historical knowledge. His good looks didn't hurt either. Silently, she reprimanded, *Get a grip, chica*. She mustn't let herself be captivated, no matter the guy's charm and attractiveness. Her mission was to suss out what the enemy was up to. Nothing more. "He's trouble," Marty had cautioned—only knowing the half of it, she suspected. Or, more likely, familiar as he was with Nina's weakness for rogues, Marty might have been warning her off for that very reason as well.

She knew about the demolition, certainly. Fascinated but sad to see it destroyed, she'd held a mesmerized five-year-old Raul in her arms and stood together with neighbors who gathered from a distance to watch the building implode when the battering ball ripped into its side. Marty's recent title search documented the court order for the demolition, along with revealing a bundle of ancient and recent liens, claims on the building for delinquent taxes, and water, trash, and sewer charges. All were requiring complicated, expensive untangling. Marty had thrown the files to a couple of eager third-year law school summer interns to figure out. *Pro bono*, of course. Were it not for Marty, the gardeners risked getting what they paid for. Nothing. Paying for the work was out of the question. But she knew Marty wouldn't let them down. He'd see to it the kids did the job right, and he'd help find a fix no matter what it took.

Nina wasn't about to share any of this with Ace Moon. Let him think the gardeners were angelic lambs doing good works, helping the neighborhood. Nor would she reveal anything about Marty's high-powered law firm and her own political connections at work behind the scenes. She wouldn't hesitate to use their do-good innocence later, to shame Ace if he turned out indeed to be the enemy. She needed to find out what he was up to. Giving him her sweetest smile, she decided to engage him further in discussion of more history facts, in hopes he'd divulge his motives and game plan directly.

Ace spoke first though, completely throwing her off balance. "You're pretty interesting too, Counselor," he remarked cunningly. "Please, Nina. Don't feign surprise. It's not like your face isn't in the *Chronicle* every other week. Someone in my line of work always has an eye out for a good defense lawyer, and by all counts, you're the best in town. Let's cut the pretense. You don't wear it well at all. I know your peeps sent you over to check me out. You want to know why I'm here? It must be obvious. The lot's come on the tax sale list, and I plan to buy it."

Nina was stunned by this disclosure. That he wanted the lot wasn't the curveball. Rather, how'd the lot get onto the tax sale rolls? Was Ace bluffing? Trying to call out their strategy so he could undermine it?

Only weeks before, she'd gotten a handshake agreement from City Supervisor Riley. Now she kicked herself for not getting the promise in writing, and wished she could kick the politician for not honoring his word. He had definitely implied that as long as they did their due diligence and had the money to buy it, the lot was theirs. He'd told her that he would see to it that the lot stayed off the tax sale rolls until the end of the year. Had Ace gotten to him, or to someone more powerful higher up the food chain?

"Well, clearly there's a mistake," huffed Nina. "The garden's not for sale."

Nina stood straight in her heels and put her hands on her hips, trying to appear more unshakeable than warranted by either her petite, 5'1" stature or the supervisor's flimsy promise. Ace grinned; Nina knew a "gotcha" when she saw one.

"But it will be for sale at the tax sale this December. And I will be there," he said.

How could she be so stupid? The tax sale was to happen in December? Had she misunderstood Riley? Nina clenched her fists. Mute white heat filled her. Afterward, Nina would torment herself with a replay of every word that passed between them, especially how she succumbed so easily to her stupefying rush of fury, embarrassment, and…desire, as those laughing, unflinching green eyes bored into hers.

"Hey listen, Nina," Ace said. "Everyone's talking about the new chef at the Top of the Mark. How about we discuss all of this more up there? Eight o'clock, Saturday? On me, of course. Right now, it looks like this little show is about to start, and that's my cue to be off."

Speechless, Nina scowled at Ace as he walked away. Stepping through the garden arch, he casually turned back in her direction, waved, and shouted, "Game's on, babe!"

In an uncustomary and unwelcome fog, she stumbled toward the nearest hay bale where she collapsed and willed herself to get a grip. It didn't help her composure when Allegra and her friends whizzed by, heading toward the back of the stage, their mouths open and chirping like swallows.

MR. ADAMS

M r. Adams turned and watched Allegra's zany flight toward the stage with her friends. His heart clenched when he heard Liz exclaim as they ran past her, "I love you, Allegra Stevenson." How deeply he felt the same. *I've fallen in love with that little girl, with this garden, and…all of it. So how come I feel so down today?*

Mr. Adams had felt his mood shift as soon as he left Lotte's side, and his despair seemed to worsen at what should have been the joyful sight of Allegra. Depression would be the obvious diagnosis if he were to seek a professional opinion, something he was not about to do. He'd had his fill of specialists in those agonizing months of recovery after the accident. Other than periodic check-ups with his GP that were mandated by the school department as part of his employment, Mr. Adams preferred to stay clear of the medical world. Discharge from rehab meant, for him, a kind of graduation back into what he could piece together as a life. He was freed from the clutches of overly cheerful, well-meaning physical therapists, occupational therapists, mental health therapists, art therapists, and nurses and doctors who'd probed into every orifice of his body. It took vigilant effort to keep them from intruding into the wounded byways of his mind too. No, he was better off on his own than with someone who, even with good intentions, would inevitably drag him into revisiting those dark days. Nothing was to be gained by brooding over debilitating, painful memories.

Mr. Adams knew from experience that what usually worked best when guilt threatened to rip his sanity was to stay busy with his hands, making or fixing something. His job as a janitor reliably kept him busy with an endless stream of things to repair or clean around the school. At home, too, he always had a project underway in his wood shop to keep his mind from spiraling downwards. In the past few months, the community garden drew his hands and...heart to more positive possibilities than he'd dared imagine for many years.

Surveying the happily chaotic scene around him, he should have felt happier to be there. Here were his neighbors, people who he'd passed for years on the street, at the corner store, waiting for the bus. Once faceless to him, today they greeted each other by name and stopped to talk. Sufficient reason to feel upbeat. But he didn't, at all.

The garden, in its early summer bloom, beckoned him into its center. In hopes of distracting himself, Mr. Adams strolled away from the people who were gathering around the stage. He noticed the wildflowers he and Allegra seeded in the rubble along one edge of the garden had taken hold. They were beginning to flower amid a fine crop of hardy perennial weeds. A new perimeter bed ready for more wildflowers stretched around the other three sides of the garden. It too would be planted soon, once restored from the day's mole trampling. All 20 of the gardeners' raised beds were overflowing with plants. The Alvarez family, which included six children, had two beds, one dedicated entirely to a monocrop of tomatoes. Despite Mr. Adams's warning that tomatoes would not ripen in the Mission's foggy weather, they'd fashioned a make-shift greenhouse with a draped plastic sheet over bent tubing. Mr. Adam gently lifted a corner of the plastic and was gratified to behold hundreds of tiny yellow blossoms, proving his prophecy wrong and foretelling a bountiful early harvest.

The sight of Lotte and Allegra's garden bed, a

hilarious study in bio-intensive diversity, brought an authentic smile. In their 4-by-12 space they'd crammed no fewer than ten varieties of vegetables. He counted potatoes, cabbage, lettuce, green peppers, chili peppers, eggplant, sweet peas, carrots, and radish, snuggled tightly with thyme, basil, marigolds, calendula, and larkspur, each plant with its own label. An exuberant pumpkin vine wandered over the edge of their bed into the pathway between their bed and his.

The box on the other side of his own yielded a different aesthetic. Gardened by Josie and Paulo, their bed was tidy with gourmet salad greens—a gorgeous blend of green and purple cut-and-regrow varieties that were lovely to behold. Next to their bed, Mr. Adams noticed that Nina's marigolds and beans were coming along. Early in the season she'd asked him for advice, confessing she had no time to maintain much of anything. He could see that his tip about spreading a thick layer of leaf mulch around the plants to hold back weeds seemed to be working.

Mr. Adams's thoughts strayed to the backyard of his family's hillside home in Bernal Height, where, at his father's feet, he'd learned to love working the good soil. Although Mr. Adams's father, much to his mother's irritation, was habitually uncommunicative inside the house, outside he was more talkative, instructing his son with gentleness and ease about the care of vegetables, fruit trees, and flowers in their sheltered backyard.

He reconnected with his love of gardening years later, when he built plant boxes for his flat's first floor windows overlooking the street. His seasonally changing mix of primrose, nasturtium, basil, thyme, chrysanthemum, and sedum turned out to be a pretty dependable antidote to melancholy. Accustomed to solitude, Mr. Adams was surprised that he found he enjoyed the human connections the window boxes inspired. Often, while he tended the boxes, passersby stopped to show their appreciation and chat. Willie, his next-door neighbor, asked Mr. Adams to build matching boxes for his windows, too—all the more remarkable, because this was their first communication in over 10 years of living side by side. Next thing he knew, a teacher from Moscone Elementary School two blocks down enlisted Mr. Adams's aid in building two small raised-bed boxes for a vegetable and flower garden she wanted to plant with her third-graders on the school grounds.

He later learned that it was Lotte who had tucked a flier into the soil of one of his window boxes. That's how he first heard about the neighborhood families who wanted to turn the nearby vacant lot into a community garden as a source of food and companionship. He, Lotte, and Mrs. Hatfield were the only people who attended that first meeting, where, unable to respond otherwise in the face of Lotte's forceful persuasion, he reluctantly agreed to serve as president for the Garden Planning Committee.

Mr. Adams enjoyed sharing his knowledge about gardening, but as president he was often consulted about garden affairs that had more to do with people than plants, something he felt he knew little about. Sometimes he got lucky, though. Earlier that morning, for instance, when Antoine asked him what to do about their box while they were away for the coming year, an impromptu thought produced a perfect solution. Mrs. Hatfield's grandson, Neilson, and his wife, Emma, were happy to take over Antoine's garden and the vegetables through the season.

However...Mr. Adams shook his head in dismay as he gazed at Henry Swanson's raised bed. Here was a problem he certainly had no idea how to resolve. Swanson, a retired shipyard welder, was creating an as-yet-undefined work-in-progress. Recently his crisscrossing of bedsprings, rusted plumbing fixtures, and other *"junque,"* as Henry referred to it, had expanded and was overgrowing the boundaries of Henry's raised bed, reaching toward others' and filling considerable air space above it. Very soon, Henry would need to install supports in the pathways outside of his garden to hold up the structure, and some of Henry's neighbors were not happy about losing access to the pathways.

As if on cue, Nate Billings, one of Henry's fiercest critics, stood up from kneeling in the midst of his fastidiously manicured box next to Henry's. "You got to stop Henry, John."

Mr. Adams sighed. He bent to deadhead one of Billing's exotic succulents, which were precisely labeled with their Latin names on metal signs, as if to showcase a botanical garden. He reminded Nate of the Committee's unanimous decision for the garden to have an open spirit. Anyone could grow anything in their boxes as long as it wasn't toxic, like chemicals for pest control or illegal weeds. Seeing Nate's frown, Mr. Adams could see he wasn't buying it.

"Get real, Adams! 'Anything goes' shouldn't include junk. And that is J-U-N-K," he spelled, for emphasis. "He doesn't have one plant in there."

Mr. Adams pointed to the barely seen, wilted clematis vine that Henry had planted at the base of his *objet d'art*. Nate guffawed and Mr. Adams had to agree that the sculpture was certainly outgrowing the vine. He also found himself agreeing with Nate's point that the acetylene torch Henry used was stretching the chemical ban too far, so he promised to ask Henry to weld pieces off site. But he knew that, like the zucchini vines in Mrs. Hatfield's garden, Henry's work was clearly in a growth spurt with no end in sight. Compromise would appease no one.

Mr. Adams saw an opportune, if temporary, way out as Robin, his former student, appeared. When Robin asked for a moment, Mr. Adams promised Nate again that he'd talk to Henry and was relieved to see Nate tip his cap in a friendly gesture before taking his leave.

"What's up?" Mr. Adams asked Robin.

"Mr. A., can you look after my little cousin?" Robin nudged the thin, pasty-faced teenager who was slouching next to him. "This here is Jake"

Mr. Adams guessed he was middle-school age, maybe fourteen. The boy was dressed in wide-legged black jeans held up with a metal chain instead of a belt, a baggy, worn, black T-shirt under a stretched-out black hoodie, and scuffed, lace-up combat boots. Mr. Adams tried to avoid giving undue attention to the metal ring in the boy's nose and extended his hand. The boy kept his heavy-lidded eyes lowered and his hands pocketed. Mr. Adams sighed, knowing whatever was being asked of him would entail something complicated.

Robin must have sensed his hesitation because before he could reply, Robin blurted his case quickly. "Jake's got in a little trouble, but he's a good kid. He needs to work off 20 hours of community service. Can he do it with you maybe? Please?"

"Ah…" Mr. Adams was inclined to refuse. The

boy's demeanor hardly gave enthusiastic support to his cousin's blatantly exaggerated recommendation. Jake was not anyone's idea of a "good kid," by a long shot. But when a drumroll called the milling crowd to the stage, Mr. Adams relented. Wasn't today supposed to be about celebrating the magnificent wonder of all that is happening in this garden? He reckoned there had to be room here for this troubled teenager.

"All right." Mr. Adams looked directly at Jake, though the boy didn't raise his eyes from the ground. "If you don't show, even once, the deal is off. Understand?" Sternly he instructed, "Tomorrow morning then, eight sharp. On second thought, you can start right now, clocking hours by sitting through today's garden show."

Robin thanked him profusely, repeating that the kid wasn't bad, he merely wanted people to think he was tough to protect himself. Mr. Adams noted Jake's wordless response was to kick a wad of dirt with the toe of his massive boot. *The world's in shambles*, thought Mr. Adams as the weight of familiar despair returned. If only he could bury his face in the solace of Lotte's shoulder, as he'd seen Liz do earlier...but not a muscle moved in Lotte's direction. Instead, he positioned Jake and Robin on a bale of hay that was placed near the garden's arch, far enough away from the action for them to maintain a comfortable distance. Then, he pasted a smile on his face like a mask and proceeded closer to the stage, confident no one near him would detect the unshakeable pall dragging him down. By the time he made his way closer to the stage, the seats near Lotte and Liz were filled. A disappointment…although, given his current state of mind he thought it just as well to take a straw bale at the outside edge of the gathering beside Henry.

Mr. Adams watched as Josie came from behind the flimsy satin curtain onto the stage. She wore a low-cut evening gown in bluish green and held a silver wand tipped with a tinsel foil covered star. A garland of fresh daisies and freesias crowning her hair completed her costume. Waving, she greeted the crowd to the sound of an admiring whistle.

An unfeigned smile flickered across Mr. Adams' face as he deduced that the whistle must surely have come from Paulo. He spotted Josie's long-time partner dressed in a pea-green tuxedo with a splashy, turquoise sash arrayed across his chest. He was also sporting a jaunty crown of yarrow and poppies fit for the garden's royalty. Parked in a wheelchair next to Lotte, Paulo's bone-thin face was radiant. Josie posed flirtatiously and blew a kiss to Paulo, causing the audience to clap in delight.

Then, with a grandiose pose, Josie announced, "It is my exquisite pleasure to welcome you to the garden, to our garden." She paused for more applause, which went on until she gestured with an exaggerated movie style slash across the throat for them to stop so she could continue. "As you know, all over the country today people are celebrating Independence Day. But here on the corner of Chula and Abby, we recognize a different reality: Inter-dependence Day."

Mr. Adams watched Josie playing to her crowd of gardeners, neighbors, their friends, and family. A rallying cry moved the audience to take up the spirited words, "Inter-United, we grow! Inter-United we grow!"

As the chant ended, Josie shook her head in mock sincerity and placed her right hand on her breast, "Ah yes. Give peas a chance." Then she hiked up her dress revealing a brilliant scarlet garter belt, and kicked out one long hairy leg. "What do we say? We say, We do what we can-can." As many groans as laughs followed. "But right now...drumroll, please. It is my distinct honor to announce that...I can't hold back mis-quoting a bit of Shakespeare here, sorry Pablo...'We few, we happy few, we band of brothers' and of course, sisters...we of the magnificent beginnings of the Chula Lane Community Garden today celebrate the in...in... ineffable mystery of our inter-connectedness with all beings. Ineffable? Did I get that right, Lotte?"

Mr. Adams watched Lotte give two thumbs up to Josie's usage as the speech continued.

"And we hereby give official recognition to the passage of the sixth year in Ms. Allegra Stevenson's already remarkable life. Born today, the Fourth of July, a full six years ago. Please welcome our very own Allegra, worm-wrangler extraordinaire. Please come to the stage!"

The sound of the drum increased, and Josie looked expectantly toward the fluttering satin sheet on one side of the stage. When no one appeared, Mr. Adams was quick to his feet, concerned that something had happened to Allegra.

Josie called, "Yoo-hoo, Ms. Allegra, could you come out for a moment? We have something to sing to you. *Hoo hoo hoo hoo hoo*," crooned Josie. Mr. Adams recognized the schmaltzy notes of the old song, "An Indian Love Call."

Still no Allegra. Mr. Adams was about to check backstage to see if everything was all right when he saw Allegra's face peeking from behind the curtain. He could tell she was scared by the way she bit her lip and he wished he could make it easier somehow. Josie gave an encouraging wave, and Allegra tiptoed slowly and carefully toward her. Hands waved and clapped in encouragement. Nina's son, Raul, shouted, "Tight, dude." Mr. Adams held his breath as Allegra hesitated, then walked to the middle of the stage.

Halfway through the crowd's rendition of "Happy

Birthday," Allegra reached out her hand for Josie to hold, and Mr. Adams felt a pain stab inside his chest. He reached for the handkerchief in his back pocket to blow his nose. What was going on? Tears? It couldn't be. He was not a crier. Even when he'd had everything to cry about, he hadn't. He'd not shed a single tear, even when he learned that his wife Marjorie and baby Julia's caskets were lowered into the earth as he lay in hospital, barely conscious and in constant pain. Thank God for Marjorie's parents, Julia's grandparents—they took care of everything. Mr. Adams's mind continued to speed along the well-worn path of the tragedy. Once home from the hospital, he'd come close to tears. When he finally visited the shaded hillside of Oakland's Bayview cemetery, grass grew thickly atop two parallel grave mounds. Numbed from grief, no tears fell…then, or since.

Mr. Adams forced his attention back to the event stage. It was unclear to him what was happening there, but then he realized he probably would have been none the wiser had he been following the action more closely. A harpist played an eerie, free-form waltz, and several children dressed in flowing, sequined costumes swooped in and out of each other's way across the stage. Some bobbed up and down holding little Japanese parasols in each hand. Streams of bubbles accompanied by children's giggles filtered gently down on the audience. Several children flapped their arms like wings and made eerie, bird-like calls. He spotted Allegra easily. It took a moment to guess what part she was playing, but then he figured it out...she (barely) resembled the worm she was pretending to be by writhing on her belly in a gunny sack costume.

The sight of Allegra suddenly made it impossible for Mr. Adams to deny the crushing ache inside his chest. As discreetly as possible, he stood and walked out of the garden. He left with no destination in mind but soon found himself making his way across the bay to Oakland, to the cemetery where Marjorie and Julia were buried. The Market Street bus was at its stop when he rounded the corner. He boarded, grateful to bypass the hapless drama of panhandlers, drunks, and prostitutes outside the 24th and Mission BART Station.

As Mr. Adams rode quietly in the near-empty bus along Valencia Street he warmed to the beautiful day, the kind of San Francisco afternoon that takes on an otherworldly glow, seeming to light even shadows from within. He admired the light's play on the passing color wheel of buildings—a large, stucco apartment painted in pumpkin with teal green trim, its neighbor a purple storefront with bright orange lettering: "La Bodega." Tempered by the afternoon's golden light, he found even the most garish combinations arresting.

When he reached Market Street and descended the escalator, luck was on his side again. Like the bus, the train to Oakland was there waiting for him. Once there, he took the bus along College Avenue to Piedmont Avenue, bringing him to the cemetery within the hour. At the entrance, Mr. Adams let his architect's eye wander over the contours of the distinctive, redwood-sided chapel designed by Berkeley's famous architect Julia Morgan. Mr. Adams spotted Sue and Tom where they sat behind their small flower stand to the left of the big, wrought-iron gateway. *Rain or shine, they are here*, he thought. He was glad to see them and knew they expected him to stop for a visit. His last trip was three months earlier.

Year upon year, he'd come dutifully. Except for interacting with his students and coworkers at the high school during the week, and an occasional woman friend on a date that amounted to little, Mr. Adams kept to himself. Until the garden, the only people he spoke with on weekends were salespeople at the markets where he shopped, or at the diner around the corner. When he did visit the cemetery, he always bought flowers from Sue and Tom's small market. Their displays featured each season's specialty—at Easter it was potted lilies, for Thanksgiving a harvest theme, and pine wreaths for Christmas. Today there were mini American flags on wooden sticks, along with buckets of red, white, and blue gladiolas and dried flower arrangements to honor the soldiers on the Fourth of July.

Gesturing to the flags, Tom invited Mr. Adams to take one and queried, "You okay, John? It's been a long time since you've been here."

Mr. Adams put his hands up and smiled to signal that, though grateful, he wouldn't take advantage of their generosity.

Sue insisted, "It's okay, our gift. America! Take!"

So Mr. Adams did a quick bow, selected one of the flags, and thanked her. He held it awkwardly, then carefully wound the flag around its pole and placed it in his jacket pocket. "Happy Fourth."

The war...entering the cemetery gates, Mr. Adams thought about the fact that every US generation seemed to have its own war. His was the Vietnam War. Sue and Tom, now very Americanized, were refugees from that war.

He was 21 and about to enter graduate school in architecture when the draft started up. Such a long time ago—he remembered his ambition as if it were someone else's life. Combat wasn't an option. When he learned that his draft number was low, he was certain he would be called up soon. His mother said he didn't have the bravery for war, but his father

KATHERINE H. BROWN

acknowledged his bravery for resisting. No matter what, he knew he couldn't kill.

Besides, no one could explain to his satisfaction what we were doing there in the first place. He toyed with the idea of training as a medic, but in the end, sat down and wrote a CO application, logically building his case. Thankfully, his draft board granted the exemption. He put his heart and passion into a day program for addicted teens and worked nights with the war resistance. Fueled by the energy and optimism of the dedicated draft counselors, he felt useful most of the time. However, the sheer weight of people's plight would often overwhelm him, and he would retreat for a while into himself. Until Marjorie...

An insistent tat-tat-tat of a woodpecker brought Mr. Adams's awareness from the past. His eyes scanned up the hill, overlooking the cemetery to a row of four tall Canary Island palms edged by a grove of Monterey pines and the red bushy blooms of bottlebrush shrubs. Over the years, Mr. Adams often bypassed the cemetery's headstones and the sad stories they told, and instead hiked to this wooded hilltop, his painful body be damned. There, he'd make a nest in the knee-deep grasses under two giant eucalyptus trees. Songbirds competed for his attention with the distant flow of freeway traffic sounding like the muted roar of a giant river. When the winds blew clear and bright off the ocean, he could enjoy a panoramic view of Lake Merritt and Oakland's downtown to the south, and the spire of the University of California's campanile to the north. Beyond the harbor's huge container ships and arching cranes to the west were Treasure Island, the long reach of the Bay Bridge, and San Francisco's skyscrapers. Mount Tam to the north kept vigil over the distant coming and going of boats and ferries moving in the sapphire bay below.

Forswearing the cemetery's heights this time, instead Mr. Adams found his feet taking him along the smaller road that forked to the right, away from the sign for the columbarium, the Home of Eternity. He passed the section of the graveyard reserved for Temple Israel and took a right as the road branched and climbed steeply uphill, where headstones of granite chiseled with Chinese calligraphy stood. Occasionally, he'd seen visitors burn offerings in the red-painted cans provided near these graves, but this day, no one was there.

Higher up on the right side of the road, Mr. Adams saw an elderly man with his arm over a woman's shoulder. She was crying into a handkerchief held to her eyes. Nearby, a man and two women sat on a red, plaid blanket surrounded by food. "You're it!" called a child as she tagged another in play. A ways beyond, Mr. Adams noticed a military headstone and stopped.

The stone read "Dennis Turner June 28, 1932 - July 23,1953. Purple Heart."

Echoing the child's words, he whispered, "You're it." He took the little flag from his pocket, stood it in the grass beside the stone, and murmured, "Happy Fourth of July, soldier."

Where the road curved left, Mr. Adams walked onto the grass past a carved marble angel, a pint-sized version of Allegra. Ten feet beyond, he stopped in front of two plain granite stones resting side by side. "Remembered in Love" was carved into the stone face of each, under which were the names of the two people he loved most in all the world. Their death dates and resting places were shared: February 10, 1974.

He dropped to the ground on his knees, compelled by an irresistible force. Then, as if felled by a strong wind, he lay face down into the grass, crossways over both graves. Self-conscious that he must appear like some zealous pilgrim, he grimaced and struggled to get up, but his strength drained inexplicably, leaving him helpless. Silence surrounded him, broken only by the steady percussion of his heart pounding in his chest. He breathed deeply and helplessly, surrendering his body to the ground beneath. His fingers length-ened so that his palms lay flat in the cool dampness of the grass. Motionless, he lay there until his hands and arms began to tingle in a pleasant if unfamiliar way. Inexplicably, he gave way to the impulse to place his lips on the tips of grass blades below his face, and he began to kiss the grass. Laughing, he dotted the ground with many more kisses, enjoying the sweet green smell of freshness from the grass and the absurdity of what was happening beyond his control.

As unexpectedly, tears followed next. His body convulsed with waves of guilt for not saving wife and child, for taking them on that trip, on that road, at that moment. Why hadn't he died too? Why was he still here? Shattered by intense pining for what couldn't be, he squeezed his eyes shut. They were lost to him forever. Oh, that he too could slip into the darkness that waited for him under the grass. He longed to enter there, yearned to curl into its stillness and join with the roots, stones, and sightless creatures of the underworld. Asking that the earth's surface to part open and let him in, he was answered by silence.

In the course of time, the irritation of a pebble under one knee grew unbearable, and he rolled onto his back. He sighed, pulled a handkerchief from his pocket, and blew his nose. He re-folded the cloth carefully and placed it on the ground. A breeze stirred the acacia's branches above him, drawing attention to the flickering patterns created by quaking leaves against the blue of the sky.

A wordless understanding replaced his despair. With intense certainty, he knew he wouldn't need to return to the cemetery for a long while. Marjorie and Julia had already moved on. Where had they gone? There was no answer to this question, other than his conviction that they would always remain in the realm of his heart. It was time for him to move on, too.

But where to, and how will I ever get there? he wondered.

Then he felt Marjorie's presence, soft and fleeting as a gentle glance, and the way forward was clear. He imagined her sweet laughter and her promise: "Darling, let the world love you again, and all will be right."

LOTTE

otte touched Allegra's forehead lightly with her lips. She watched the child open her eyes, scoot over in bed to give her room to sit, and, in a not-at-all sleepy voice, ask, "Lotte?"

"D'you have fun today, sugar?"

"Best birthday ever!" exclaimed Allegra, sitting up abruptly.

Lotte reached unsuccessfully for the comforter before it fell entirely off the bed.

"I had more cakes than anybody. Mrs. Hatfield gave me three kinds. I gave the vanilla frosting to the worms because I only liked the chocolate."

"I'll bet they enjoyed that."

"Oh yes," answered Allegra.

Lotte watched the child's smile become a frown and asked, "What's up, Pigeon?"

"Lotte? D'you think worms mind I don't use their real names?"

"What do you mean?"

"There are too many. I can't tell which one is Godfrey anymore. I can't tell them apart."

"Hmmm. I see the problem. Do you think they mind?"

"I don't know. That's how come I asked *you*."

Amused by Allegra's sassy impatient comeback, Lotte watched the child fold her arms in front of her chest and kick a stuffed rabbit onto the abandoned comforter on the floor. Picking the rabbit from the floor and cradling it on her lap, Lotte asked, "Do you mind when I don't use your real name?" She pulled up the comforter too, and gently re-covered Allegra under it.

"Sometimes. Most times it's okay. Only when you call me Piglet. I hate that."

"Well, then. I certainly won't call that name ever again." Lotte paused, hoping Allegra was assured by her promise. "Would you like to know why I call you names like Larkspur and Peapod?" Allegra nodded; Lotte continued, "Well, when you were born, I looked at you in your tiny bed in the hospital and…" Lotte's eyes filled with tears as she remembered Allegra swaddled in her tiny bassinet in the hospital's nursery. It was her first sight of the child, and she often returned to this memory of the utter purity of her joy in that moment.

"You were sooo bee-u-tiful."

Allegra's feet wormed their way under her as the child scrunched deeper under the comforter.

"You had the pinkest little bud of a mouth and the smoothest skin. And your hair was so thick and soft. And sooo dark." Implicitly noting the contrast, Lotte patted her own head of graying hair. "You had sweet little wavy curls all over." Lotte loved the twinkle in Allegra's eye and her grin as she warmed to the description. "Child, I'd never seen anything as precious. I was alone with you and the other newborn babies lying in their baby-sized beds. Your mama was asleep down the hall in her room, as, I guess, were the other mamas too. It was late at night, like now. The nursery was warm as toast and the lights were dim. You were asleep, but every so often you would kind of do this with your lips."

As Lotte knew she would, Allegra giggled when she moved her tongue gently between her lips. "Maybe you were hungry?" Then Lotte started kissing the air. "Or sending kisses to the angels?"

"That's funny, Lotte. But then what happened?"

Lotte cleared her throat and took two sustained

breaths to center herself before continuing. The memory of that night always stirred her heart profoundly. When she spoke her voice was soft.

"I saw you in your crib there in the hospital…and I was aware of what every grandmother in our family felt the first time they beheld their precious grandbaby sleeping. I felt my own grandmother was there with us, smiling at us. And her grandmother before, and on back as far back as forever. Hmmm…they all came tumbling in.

"It was like all the grandmothers were there with me and you in the nursery. You can imagine the room got pretty crowded with all those grandmothers. All those grandmothers from everywhere, from all time, they were gazing and cooing ever so gently as you lay sleeping."

Lotte laughed as Allegra sat up in bed again, her eyes wide and clearly delighted. She took in another deep breath and let it out in a long sigh as she eased Allegra's head back onto the pillow. She brought her face close to Allegra's and breathed in the sweet innocence of the child's natural scent.

She whispered, "There we all were, looking down at you. Me and all the grandmothers looking over my shoulders. Yes, so happy to see your puckered-up little face. Well then!" Lotte said in hushed tones of excitement while sitting up and lightly clapping her hands together. "We were all kinds of grandmothers crowding around. There were moth and mosquito grandmothers, geranium grandmothers, and pine tree grandmothers." Lotte counted on her fingers, one by one, each new kind of grandmother. "...And chicken grandmothers, giraffe grandmothers, ladybug grandmothers, and for sure, gladiola grandmothers."

"For true?" Allegra asked, eyes sparkling.

"Absolutely true. Every word." Lotte put her first finger up to her lips and held it there for a time, not sure how to continue. Then it was clear.

"See? When I call you Pinecone, Turtle Dove, or any other name like that, I'm speaking for the grandmothers who can't, but who would call you that name if only they could. Pine trees and pea plants have no mouths, do they? And bumblebees and wrens have no words, at least words we can understand." Lotte wanted to convey to the child the power of the insight born that night in her hospital nursery... of the boundless joy she felt in connection with all grandmothers because of Allegra's arrival. "You see, they love you the same as they love their own. It's like they're speaking through me to you when I call out their names for you...because you are their grandbaby too." Lotte brought the palm of her hand up to her heart. "Just like all their grandbabies are mine."

"For true?" asked Allegra.

Lotte sensed Allegra's confusion and responded, "Doesn't make much sense, does it? Are some things best left a mystery, I wonder…hmmm." Lotte stilled herself to listen inside until a certainty arose. "There's no mystery in it. It is simply a truth. You are grand-baby to every grandmother, and they'll take care of you with as much love as for their own. And their children are mine to care for as I will for you, always."

"You really don't know any of this for real, huh, Lotte?"

"That's right, no evidence for sure," Lotte con-fessed, faced with the child's surprising skepticism. She stood up and gave one more kiss to Allegra's forehead, but then corrected herself. "But I do know it's true, my Darlin' Dandelion. Maybe we don't get to know some things with our heads. A lot's unknowable in that sense. Like, where do dreams go when we wake up in the morning? But other things, like me telling you how much I love you? Well, you and I both know in our hearts that that's true, right? How's that for a puzzle to nod off with…hmmm?"

Lotte reached over and turned off the light by Allegra's bed. She walked over to the door and turned. "Goodnight, Allegra, my dear. Thanks for telling me about Piglet. Promise you'll let me know if any other names bug you?"

Lotte's heart swelled as she heard Allegra's faint reply spoken into the darkness. "I promise."

FALL

Many arrivals make us live: ...
a seed pushing itself beyond itself,
the mole making its way through darkest ground,
the worm, intrepid scholar of the soil...

The body moves, though slowly, toward desire.
We come to something without knowing why.

Theodore. Roethke, The Manifestation in (1964). *The Far Field*. Doubleday.

LOTTE

The desk phone rang as Lotte placed a framed photograph of Allegra and Liz into her briefcase to give to Vince when they met for lunch. The phone clicked over to her message machine and a man's voice came from the little black box.

"Hello, Lotte?"

"Mr. Adams?" said Lotte as she picked up the phone.

"John's fine, but yes...ah, this is John Adams."

"Hi, I..." Lotte hesitated. Calling him John still did not trip lightly from her lips. "...John, of course. You're calling about Allegra?"

"Yes. I was on the phone with Liz a minute ago and she suggested I give you a ring to find out when to drop her by."

Lotte wedged the phone receiver beneath her chin to have both hands free. She zipped her briefcase closed while she explained that she'd be home by six o'clock following her lunch in Oakland. They agreed that he would pick Allegra up from school and they'd spend time in the garden before having a snack around the corner in the Morning Diner.

"And you're sure this is okay?" asked Lotte "I'll probably be home before, if you want to check back earlier."

"No, no. It'll be fun. Not to worry," said Mr. Adams, "I don't have anything on for tonight until 7:30, the garden meeting in the church basement."

Lotte thanked him. It wasn't the first time he'd stepped up to help, and it meant a lot to her. During the summer, Lotte had no problem taking in Allegra overnight when Liz worked a late shift at the restaurant. But once September came, Liz's boss gave her two late shifts working as a waitress and steady billing every Friday night with the house band. So, in a pinch, Liz asked Mr. Adams to fill in for Lotte, and he was always obliging.

"My pleasure," said Mr. Adams. Then he took Lotte aback by introducing another topic. "By the way. I've meant to tell you how much I liked your article in *Harper's*."

"You saw it?" asked Lotte, pleased, but caught off

guard as she found herself adjusting her image of this Mr. Adams. Who was he anyway...reading *Harper's Magazine?*

She couldn't claim to be unaware of Mr. Adam's attentiveness. Months earlier, Lotte was bemused when Liz accused her of wanting more than a platonic relationship with him. Though she'd protested that she enjoyed the same polite, formal, and gently humorous manner Mr. Adams used with everyone, more and more she was aware of subtle, but telling cues. She may have misjudged the situation. Despite his usual reserve with people, he did seem to be going out of his way to look out for Allegra's well-being, who he obviously adored, and who adored him. And he was certainly considerate about supporting Liz's recovery and quick to respond at the moment she, Liz, or Allegra needed something. Nonetheless, from her side, Lotte carefully kept it light between them, while appreciating his shared affection for her family and the garden. Keeping a distance felt like the safer route. Now this surprise. It had never occurred to Lotte that Mr. Adams would be interested in her work and what she wrote, or that she'd be so taken by his praise.

"Inspired me to fire off a letter to my senators about the Farm Bill," Mr. Adams.... *John* said, to her delight.

"You did?"

"Absolutely. You made such a good case. I bet a lot of people will do the same."

"You think so?" Lotte asked, one eyebrow raised.

"I know so. The strength of the article is not solely your research on hunger, but the way you personalized your struggle about what to do."

Captured by his engaging observation, Lotte admitted to him that she'd stepped out of her comfort zone by positioning her argument in such a personal way. "I'm glad you think it worked."

"It more than worked. That's why it wasn't simply another academic article on hunger. It was about us, your readers, and recognizing our sense that we're powerless to do anything. Your point, it seemed to me, is that our impotence is merely a trap of perception. Change our minds, we change the world."

Lotte was thrilled that he found meaning beyond her intention—though it seemed obvious now that she heard it.

"Maybe that's why it's so powerful," he continued. "You didn't hit the reader over the head with preaching, or take us on a guilt trip. You let the reader understand what it feels like when we see someone begging or read about someone who's hungry."

As Mr. Adams paused, Lotte, even while shying away from the flattery, found she was eager to hear what he would say next.

"Then you clarified a number of options for what we can do rather than turning away from the confusion. I most admired the point you made that turning away from pain is never an answer. This is something...I've only accepted recently and continue to re-learn daily. Your article helped me along this path. I want you to know how much that means to me."

-

Still pleased and surprised by Mr. Adams's unexpected comments on her article, Lotte smiled as she climbed the three steps to a sunny restaurant terrace in Heritage Square, a refurbished office complex in downtown Oakland. She needed to return some books to the university library nearby, so she didn't mind coming across the Bay in response to Vince's request to meet him there. She was curious.

Vince was waving at her from under a soft pink umbrella that perfectly matched his oxford shirt. A man who wears pink shirts? Mr. Adams would never wear a pink shirt. Oh dear...she blushed as she caught herself thinking about him and making such a transparent comparison with her former lover.

"Lotte, the turquoise is stunning." Resisting his flattery, Lotte scoffed at his words. "And the red belt with it is perfect. You're glowing. Someone new in your life...?"

"Honestly Vince. How completely un-PC was that? Can't I just be a drop-dead gorgeous woman of a certain age without it being about some guy in my life?" She pursed her lips impatiently at Vince's sheepish expression. Though conscious she shouldn't toy with Vince's fragile ego, she couldn't resist the imp in her that enjoyed teasing him about his jealousy. So she explained that she had been seeing quite a lot of John Adams. *After all, it was true*, she thought, rationalizing the exaggeration.

"Mr. Adams? The guy in the garden? The guy Allegra's always chattering on about and believes the sun rises and sets for?"

Lotte dodged Vince as he reached for a hug. Instead, she offered a cheek one at a time to "catch" the pretentious air kisses that he sent her way. She sat down in the chair he held for her, and teased, "John and I *are* getting to be pretty good friends."

Where did this declaration come from? Did I just say what I heard myself saying?

"Hey, not all men are red-headed deviants like me," laughed Vince with a hitch in his voice. Lotte sighed. So like Vince to set her up with no good way to respond. Was she supposed to deny he's a deviant, or agree that he is? She chose neither, instead slowly and deliberately opened the menu in front of her, and redirected the conversation.

"Brazilian? It looks divine."

After ordering Salpicão chicken salad, she turned the conversation to Vince's recent move from the Midwest to Berkeley. "So, how's the move? You settling in? Need any intros? Berkeley's not Kansas anymore, Toto, as they say."

"No, I'm fine in that way, but Lotte…I do need your help with something else. I've fucked up with Liz, again. Have you talked to her this morning?"

"Why? What's wrong?" asked Lotte, her stomach clenching in dread.

"You're going to hate me," Vince said. He pulled out a monogrammed handkerchief and wiped the dampness from his forehead.

Lotte watched him finger his collar, a behavior reminiscent of other times he confessed when caught in situations which he didn't want her to discover. She held her breath, but nothing could have prepared her for what he disclosed.

"Liz is not an only child. I have another daughter. Her name is Anna," he said, barely seeming to breathe between words. Vince explained that she had phoned him.

Another daughter? Speechless, a rapid fire of unasked questions sped through Lotte's mind. *What is he talking about? The progeny of some teenage love affair? More betrayals in his past? And why in heaven's name does he bring this information to me now?* The thought of Vince having no one else with whom to share this complicated news struck her suddenly as pitiful and took the sharp edges from her anger, momentarily.

But her next breath brought a stab of anguish, as she grasped how hurtful and confusing this news would be for Liz. Lotte tasted bile and was so angry she wanted to spit. Of course this would impact Liz. No matter who she is, this new daughter of Vince's will change Liz's life. What would Liz do with this knowledge? Fear mixed with Lotte's irritation at Vince. Would Liz use this as an excuse to drink?

The revelation continued to unfold with a wrenching twist, more awful than Lotte could have imagined. "Anna and Liz are the same age, you know."

"Oh no, Vince," she muttered under her breath as it dawned on her what this signified. Vince conducted his affair when his wife was pregnant with Liz. Bowled over by this ugly fact, she said nothing. No way would she respond to Vince with his hangdog face so wishing to be soothed—or did he want to be shamed?

"I know. I know. It does seem shocking, huh?" mumbled Vince. Brightening, he added, "In a way though, I'm happy. Is that crazy?"

Oblivious to her rising anger, Vince babbled on as Lotte only half-heard his words, "Anna sounds like a well-rounded person with loving parents. She's teaching music at CAL State Hayward. I'm looking forward to getting to know her and bringing her to meet you."

To this unlikely prospect Lotte loudly exhaled, the only way she knew how to avoid pumping up Vince's melodrama. But even to this Vince responded defensively.

"I know it sounds terrible, my wife pregnant and all. But I didn't give the woman another thought after I broke it off."

That would be Vince, thought Lotte. She squelched down the temptation to leave the table before she lost all self-control and dumped her lunch, along with her not-so-ancient resentments, on this man for his womanizing and complete lack of empathy for Liz. She bit the inside of her cheek. With as much dignity as she could summon, she asked, "So what happened this morning with Liz?" She watched impatiently as Vince paid more attention to brushing off a wasp from the lip of his wine glass than answering her.

"Well, because Anna wanted to know if she had sisters, brothers…and I gave her Liz's phone number, not thinking of course."

Lotte impulsively reached across and shoved Vince's arm. The glass fell across the table leaving a red stain on the tablecloth and his pink shirt. The wasp, she noted, took off. Her response was too demure, she thought. Strangling him would have been more appropriate.

"You're pissed. I can tell," he said. "I know. I know. I've been over it a thousand times myself. I am such a fuck-up."

She would not give him the satisfaction of agreeing.

"Turns out Anna phoned Liz. And I guess Liz was pretty mean."

"Of course she was, Vince," snapped Lotte. "Can you imagine getting a call like that?"

A rigid silence lay between them. Lotte refused to fill it. *I will not put him at ease,* she swore. Let him suffer the heartache he causes so many others.

"You do hate me, don't you?"

"No. But I hate what you do."

Vince laughed, "Lotte, you're such a good Buddhist. I'm grateful to you for that and for many things."

Lotte shrugged when Vince's usual "I love you" followed. She wasn't feeling like a good Buddhist…

His next statement seemed to come out of nowhere, "Hey, I saw your article in *Harper's.* Kick-ass stuff!"

-

Replaying their dreadful conversation as the BART train swooshed into the tunnel toward home, Lotte regretted snapping back at Vince, "Yes, but did *you* write your senators?" With a sharp inhalation, Lotte closed her eyes. Not only was that Mr. Adams sneaking into her thoughts again against her better judgment, but she'd let Vince get to her repeatedly.

If she could stomp her feet and carry on like Allegra, she would have, right then and there in public. She wanted to strike out at something, someone…and then realized Vince wasn't the source of her anger. Who was the fool here? Who fell for Vince when friends warned her not to and told her she was crazy to move halfway across the country to be with him? Who but she believed him when anyone could see the liar was lying.

Lotte answered with the internal pledge not to make the same mistakes again. Mr. Adams may be a nice man devoted to Allegra, and a trustworthy babysitter, but that is who he shall remain. The garden project wouldn't be anywhere near as developed without his know-how and willingness to step up. *So I'll be cordial and open with him as I've always been, but that is all.*

No more succumbing to the folly of believing there might ever be anything more. This she promised herself, and she forced her mind to the calming sensation of her breath entering and leaving from the tip of her nose. No sooner had she relaxed when up popped an image of Mr. Adams' lips.

ALLEGRA

"Say yes! Say yes!" shouted Allegra as she bounded into Lotte's loft. Tugging on Mr. Adams's jacket pocket, she dragged him behind her through the door past Lotte.

"Lotte, pulllllleeeeeese, can Mr. Adams stay for dinner?" With the toe of one of her sneakers, she wedged the heel of the other shoe off without undoing the laces and told Mr. Adams he should take off his shoes. Mr. Adams was standing in front of Lotte, laughing. Allegra got her other sneaker off, then danced on her toes with excitement. She hurriedly explained to Mr. Adams, "Lotte doesn't like us to wear shoes inside. But she wouldn't tell you because it's not polite." Allegra looked to see Lotte's reaction and knew right away that her stern look was pretend.

Mr. Adams said to Lotte, "I must say, this is a

surprise. Honest, Lotte, I didn't put her up to begging a free meal for me."

Allegra announced, "I gotta pee," and raced to the bathroom, hoping things would work out like she planned.

When she returned, she was happy to see Mr. Adams's shoes carefully placed side-by-side next to hers beside the door. She crossed over to him and gave him her jacket to hang on an empty peg.

She sang out a big, "Thank you!" Thanks to Mr. Adams for taking her jacket, and to Lotte for saying yes.

When she returned, Lotte was in the kitchen saying, "It's slim pickings, I apologize. I've defrosted some black bean chili, and I'll make rice and a salad."

Mr. Adams said it sounded delicious. He joined Lotte by the kitchen counter and asked, "What can I do to help?"

"Me," demanded Allegra before Lotte could say anything. "Help me set the table." She reached into a drawer and counted out three forks and three spoons, then handed them to Mr. Adams.

He moved aside the pile of books and one of her drawings on the table, and asked, "Is it alright for me to clear a space here?"

Allegra nodded yes and ran back to get a hug from Lotte. "Guess what?"

"Hmmm…?" answered Lotte.

"Bandits." Allegra was aware that the "bang-bang" from the fake pistols she shot with her fingers was a bit overdramatic, but she was enjoying herself thoroughly.

"Bandits?"

"Yes. Bandits in the garden last night." Allegra flung her arms out for emphasis. "It's a mess! You should see it." Then Allegra spun a pirouette in the middle of the floor.

"Well, it's sure got you spinning, Hummingbird," said Lotte. "What's this about bandits?"

"'Bandits is what Mrs. Hatfield says, but Henry says it's the 'goddamn crack addicts.'"

"Language…" whispered Lotte, tapping her lips.

"But that's what he said!" defended Allegra, "I didn't."

"You didn't just say it?"

Feeling caught in a bind, Allegra crossed her arms in front of her chest and contested, "I was only telling you what he said."

"Understood. Tell me everything, hmmm? Bandits and crack addicts in the garden? What's this all about?"

Allegra handed Lotte the pot cover from off the counter so she could put it on top of the rice warming up on the stove. "Well," continued Allegra, "They made a huge mess in the garden. They painted 'blah-blah-blah' (what I can't say out loud) all across the stage that Josie's friends painted this summer." She wasn't about to get trapped again by telling the real words Lotte wouldn't like. "And they left the water on, so it's a huge mud puddle. Everywhere it's soaked."

"I left the hose out after watering the wildflowers," said Mr. Adams. "Someone must have turned it on again, that's all."

Allegra could tell Mr. Adams was about to add something, but she interrupted, "Let me tell. I want to tell her." She spun around to face Lotte, and said, "The worst thing of all?"

"Good heavens, what?"

"They tipped over the worm box." Allegra kicked up her heels in a quick handstand to show how the box went helter-skelter and toppled to the ground. Then she jumped back up. "And all the worms got loose."

"They all disappeared? Oh Lambkin, I am sorry."

"No," explained Allegra excitedly, "That's the good thing."

"What's the good thing?"

"See? They didn't all leave," said Allegra, still amazed that a bunch of worms were left in the upper tray. She and Mr. Adams found them munching away on some vegetable scraps and noodles she left the day before. "Some stayed, didn't they Mr. A.? I think they stayed 'cause they like it in the box. It's their home."

Mr. Adams added, "And, well, they might enjoy

it there with their very own worm wrangler, who sings to them every day and feeds them her chocolate cookies."

Allegra reported to Lotte that it was true. She'd crumpled up her cookie for them, so they wouldn't feel bad. Lotte said it was very nice of her to do this and then asked her to get the salad spinner from the drawer where it lived.

Allegra confessed, "Mrs. Hatfield gave me another. A brownie." She nudged Lotte's hip to bring her attention from the carrot she was cutting for the salad back to the garden. "And another thing?"

"Hmmm...? Don't tell me there's more?"

"Oh yes!" said Allegra, "Worms everywhere, all over, in the puddles. They can swim!" She was glad Lotte didn't know this so she could tell her also about how you're supposed to leave the worms alone when they're in puddles.

Why? Before Lotte asked, Allegra said, "Because they're looking for *mates*." Allegra carefully sounded out this new word she'd learned, then told about seeing two worms, *mating*. Talking about it felt daring, and Allegra wondered if Lotte would be mad. But she didn't look mad.

All Lotte said was, "How about that?"

So Allegra told about how the worms come up from the ground when it's wet and look for mates because their homes get stuffy, and how the rain makes it easier for them to get around. She grimaced thinking about the two worms stuck together, and told Lotte, "Mr. A. said it is very interesting, but it was gross, too."

She would have said more about it, but there was still lots more to tell Lotte about the garden. She pulled Lotte's hand. "But Lotte, guess what else?"

"I can't imagine."

"It's terrible. They pulled over Henry's gi-normous sculpture, and it crashed all over the place."

"Deus ex machina?" interrupted Mr. A., shrugging his shoulders and smiling at Lotte.

"But Henry was really, really mad," reported Allegra seriously, confused about why they were talking about machines.

"Hmmm…I'm sure he was," said Lotte. She emptied a bag of corn chips into a bowl and asked Allegra to bring napkins and three placemats. "Let's sit down with these chips while the rice simmers. And Mr. Adams…I mean, John, can you take these glasses of water?"

Allegra intervened as they reached the table, "No Lotte, you sit here." She indicated the space in between her own place and Mr. A.'s and begged, "Pullllleeeeease."

Lotte laughed and followed her instructions. "Was

anyone hurt?" she asked Mr. Adams. "Is the garden okay?"

"No one was hurt. The stage and the sculpture were both damaged, but I daresay these can be fixed pretty easily," answered Mr. Adams. "But people are upset. Henry is taking it hard."

"Oh dear," said Lotte.

Allegra asked something she wondered about before, and after today, it seemed probably true. Her pointer finger twirling beside her head, she asked, "Is Henry, you know...cuckoo?"

"No," answered Lotte, "He's an *artist*."

Then she and Mr. Adams laughed, but Allegra didn't get the joke. She pouted her lips in frustration and they stopped laughing. Mr. Adams seemed to know, like Lotte did, when she needed to say something important.

"Why do you ask, Allegra?" he asked.

"Well, today he told me I was a siren."

"I wonder what he meant," said Lotte. "Did he see you when you were singing to your worms?"

"No. And I don't know why he said it," responded Allegra, adding, "No way am I a siren."

"What did you tell him?" asked Lotte. She handed the bowl of chips to Mr. Adams and he took some in his hand.

"I didn't say anything," Allegra replied. She reached

across Lotte for the chips and said, "I went away." Then, taking a mouthful, she added, "I think he's nuts. He said the garden was a siren too."

"Ah," said Mr. Adams, "I think I know what this is about."

Lotte stood up and checked the rice on the stove.

"What do you think a siren is?" asked Mr. Adams, looking at Allegra.

"Like on a fire truck, or police, the noise it makes," she told him.

"Exactly," confirmed Mr. Adams, "Yet it has another meaning too. And I think Henry means another kind of siren." Turning to Lotte, he said, "Henry did say something about the garden being a siren, a magnet that attracts what he called 'bad elements.' He clarified he meant 'people who don't care about anyone but themselves.'" Mr. Adams shook his head, adding, "Henry wants us to put up a big fence to keep out intruders. I'm afraid the fence question will dominate the meeting tonight, right when we need to focus on so many other important things."

Allegra watched Mr. Adams raise his eyebrows and open a palm toward Lotte, who was back in the kitchen, as if inviting her to step in, "Lotte, you're the word person. Can you explain this other kind of siren?"

Lotte put the bowl of chili into the microwave and

said, "Hmmm…" like she always did before speaking. "Let me think about that while I get dinner together. Allegra, can you come get the salad? The dressing is in the fridge."

When they were all in their places at the table, Lotte said, "The kind of sirens Henry probably meant come from an ancient story. These Sirens were Greek goddesses, or spirits who lured sailors who were sailing by the Sirens' island off their boats, yes? They sang, if I remember correctly." Lotte swallowed a bite of chili and continued, "The story describes the song as incredibly seductive."

"What's see-duck-tive?" interrupted Allegra.

"It means their song was so lilting, so enchanting that it was hard…hmmm…actually, it was impossible for the sailors to resist the song's magical charm. They sailed dangerously close to the Sirens' island. The story goes that if the sailors didn't plug their ears, they would jump into the water and swim to the Sirens, leaving their boat to crash on the rocks and preventing them from ever returning home. I think that's how the story went. Gruesome when you think about it."

"That's what I remember too," added Mr. Adams. "Allegra, you'll get to read about this in a book about a hero named Odysseus. Lotte and I both read it when we were in school. All kids do."

Allegra still didn't have a clue what this book had

to do with Henry's calling her a siren. But because Mr. Adams seemed to be directing his story to her, she hung in while smearing beans around her plate, making a design of swirls and circles.

"You're wondering what this has to do with the garden, hmmm…?" asked Lotte, once again showing Allegra she could magically read her mind. "Some people, like Henry I suppose, think the garden has the power to draw, to attract things to it. Like it has a power over them. It's like a siren that's calling, reaching out, tempting people and insects and worms… everything to it, to work for it." Lotte stopped and handed the salad to Mr. Adams, who helped himself to the remaining greens. "The idea is the garden is not merely alive, but it's a strong force that gets you to do things, sometimes in a sneaky kind of way, or at least in ways that you might not be aware of."

Lotte then passed the chili dish to Mr. Adams, who settled it back onto the table and, patting his stomach, signaled he was full. He said, "Not so far-fetched actually, when you think of some of the less fun tasks required by a garden…like weeding."

"Oh," said Allegra. It was cool to think about the garden being alive. But she didn't like that the garden could make her do stuff she didn't want to do.

Mr. Adams spoke then, as if he also knew what she was thinking. "It's somewhat unsettling to think about the garden having power over me, getting me involved and concerned when I might not want to be." Allegra watched him turn to Lotte and ask, "I mean, wouldn't you feel resentful for being forced to weed?"

Lotte laughed, "Not if the garden's really good at seduction. I probably wouldn't know I was being taken in." Allegra noted Lotte's change of tone, like she was teasing him or something. "Like some fool, I might even enjoy it."

Allegra wondered if Mr. Adams would tease back. But he pulled his earlobe and said, "I suppose."

"That wasn't much of a joke, I'm sorry," said Lotte quickly. She sat back in her chair and folded her arms over her chest. "Believe me, it's taken a long time for me to find any humor in seduction."

Allegra had no idea what they were talking about, only that they were definitely not including her in their side conversation. She wondered if they would like her to get up and leave the table.

Before she could do more than think about it, Mr. Adams added, as he smiled at Lotte, "It is all fairly confusing." He shook his head. "That's an understatement. Frankly, it scares the wits out of me."

Allegra was glad to see Lotte's big smile back, but she didn't like the idea of Mr. A. being scared of anything.

Mr. Adams continued, "I'm more comfortable

thinking of the garden as a healer, not as a temptress or siren like Henry does. What is interesting though is to think about how we all project different meanings onto our experience with the garden."

"A teacher. That's what the garden is for me," said Lotte, "A good neighbor. Food pantry. Crime-stopper—though, I guess, not today…?"

"What's the garden to you, Allegra?" asked Mr. Adams.

What did she think the garden was? Feeling grown-up to be asked, Allegra took a moment before answering. *Sometimes it's like a playground,* she thought. *Other times like her best friend. A place that's fun. Home for worms and plants and the praying mantis she found with Mr. A. once, and other bugs and things.* She couldn't decide which of these to say, so she answered, "I don't know, lots of things."

It felt good to hear Lotte agree. "That garden is lots of different things, I agree. It takes all comers, giving whatever we need in return for just showing up. It's very generous, and if it is animate—*alive*—as I suspect, it must hear how silly we are, talking like this." She laughed, and Mr. Adams joined in. Allegra loved seeing them laughing together.

Checking his watch, Mr. Adams groaned. "I hope the garden keeps its sense of humor tonight." He stood up from the table and said, "My apologies, ladies. I need to leave the two of you, though I would prefer your company to this meeting. The agenda was already tricky enough, what with the details in preparation for the tax sale to save the garden. Now this 'bandit' business…"

-

When Mr. Adams left, Allegra gladly helped Lotte wash the dishes and put them away. What should she do next? She wanted to get back to her jigsaw and the bunny that had appeared in the background earlier before she had to put it away. So it was fine with Allegra when Lotte went to her desk, pulled a bunch of papers from her briefcase, and said she needed at least an hour to work on her book.

"How's *The Lies We Tell* sound to you for a title?" asked Lotte over her shoulder.

"I told a lie once." That truth slipped out of Allegra's mouth before she could stop.

"Oh…?" Lotte turned around in her chair.

"I told a lie," she repeated and looked down at her puzzle. Allegra felt Lotte's gentle eyes smiling over the top of her reading glasses.

"Do you want to tell me about it?"

"Uh-huh," answered Allegra. She sat up, pulled her legs in, and wrapped her arms around them. She dodged Lotte's eyes. "Like in your book."

"Hmmm...?"

Allegra knew from experience that Lotte was giving her time to tell her story in her own way, not getting all excited and asking nosy questions and pushing her for answers the way some grown-ups like her mom did.

When Lotte spoke softly into the silence, asking, "Lies are confusing, aren't they?" it was as though she had taken the thought right from Allegra's head. She felt okay, then, about telling the whole story, and she began slowly.

"Uh-huh. It is sort of confusing. It was back in preschool, one day. There was this doll a girl left."

"Hmmm...?"

"And I said it was mine. But it wasn't. The girl moved with her mom and dad and didn't come back, you know? But ..." She paused as she remembered. "She left her doll." Allegra rocked back and forth to calm the nervousness that started in her stomach. She clasped her knees more tightly. "And...I brought it home. And then...it broke."

She looked to find a scowl or a frown in Lotte's forehead. Finding neither, she continued, but kept an eye out in case Lotte's unwrinkled brow got stormy. "I threw it away and the teacher never found out."

"How'd you feel about that?"

"Good," admitted Allegra, a smile growing inside

her. Actually, more than good. She was very pleased, in fact. But she didn't tell Lotte that.

Lotte's nod showed she understood. "Sometimes it can be thrilling to 'get away' with a lie? Yes?"

Allegra didn't say anything. She wondered if telling only half of a story was the same as a lie.

"Lies are pretty powerful, aren't they, Lambkin?" Lotte told her. "Or some are. Pre-school was what… two years ago? It sounds like it still has a hold on you?" Allegra didn't know what Lotte meant by "a hold," until Lotte added, "It means you have remembered it for a long time. Here's what I think." Lotte leaned back in her desk chair. "Lies can stick around and haunt us because they create, maybe, a bit of guilt, along with a thrill that nobody will ever catch us. But the guilt and the thrill have a way of getting their hooks into us, and not letting go. What do you think about that?"

Allegra didn't know what she thought about anything, anymore. They were quiet for a while. Allegra liked it when Lotte asked for help to think about problems, but this time, she didn't know what to say. So she didn't say anything more.

Lotte picked up her papers, and said, "Thank you. For telling me about your lie. It means a lot that you confided in me."

"Uh-huh," answered Allegra, distracted when her eye caught the missing yellow puzzle piece she had searched for. She felt the soft snap of its fit as she pressed it into the wavy edge of what was now clearly a painted egg in the bunny's basket.

NINA

"What's an EIN?" asked Raul.

Nina smiled, leaving Marty to explain with his usual clarity the complexities of IRS employer identification numbers, who needs them and why, and the way they differ from social security numbers.

Over a delicious eggplant casserole at Marty's table, Nina was picking Marty's brain in anticipation of the upcoming garden meeting. The stakes were high, and time was running out. Legal interns at Marty's firm had completed their lengthy bureaucratic IRS application, *pro bono*. Now, with IRS approval for the garden's non-profit status, the gardeners were ready to submit Lotte's proposal asking the Community Foundation for funding to purchase the lot. Nina knew Lotte was optimistic, having heard from the foundation officer that an anonymous donor expressed specific interest in the project. But it was a big ask and there was nothing yet on paper—nor any other money in the bank. Without the foundation grant, they wouldn't stand a chance when the bidding begins at the Tax Deed Sale coming up in December.

Neither optimism, apple pie goodness, nor chance would do the trick, Marty hammered repeatedly. Dot-commers were driving a real-estate frenzy. Bidding for the lot at the tax sale in December wouldn't stop at the already whopping $150,000, which was the minimum owed the City for outstanding taxes, interest, and costs. Plus, as Marty reminded her (to her hidden chagrin), there were always greedy bottom-feeders like Ace Moon to watch out for at tax sales. People looking to make a quick buck at the expense of folks down on their luck.

"These guys' pockets are deep, and they can outbid anyone in the room by hundreds of thousands of dollars."

Ace... Nina quickly swallowed a last bite of the casserole. She gave a nod of thanks to Amy, Marty's girlfriend, and stood to clear her place—and hopefully, her mind. As of late, Ace was taking up entirely too much space in her mind. She'd just as soon make sure her face didn't give her thoughts away.

Safe at the kitchen sink with her back to the dining

room, she took up the scrub brush to rinse her plate and moved onto the stack of saucepans and mixing bowls already in the sink. Thoughts of Ace flooded her mind freely, so freely she felt her face burn. Though Ace's peck on her cheek after their picnic and walk the previous weekend might not warrant a blush, her subsequent daydreams certainly did. Despite best intentions, Nina was falling for the guy.

Of course, she'd stood him up after his outrageous Fourth of July invitation for dinner at the Top of the Mark. How dare he then show up at the League of Women Voters' annual "Women Who Could be President" Labor Day gala? She was there that evening only because, by an improbable turn of fate, she'd been chosen for their prestigious honor. Her boss mandated her presence, telling her she couldn't refuse, as it was part of the ever-expanding unwritten part of her job description as Deputy Public Defender.

In her remarks that evening, she accepted the award not for herself, but on behalf of Clara Shortridge Foltz, the barely known woman jurist who, in the 1890s, brought the concept of public defender to thirty states. When Nina finished up her speech with pointed criticism of a criminal justice system that too often rides rough with racial and gender bias on the rights of women, a few of the older, bejeweled matrons grimaced. But the majority of her listeners stood to applaud. All and all, she was feeling pretty good about the performance—until Ace edged his way through a gathering of well-wishers and turned things sweet and sour.

"Congratulations, Madam President," he said. Nina caught the admiring glance of her friend who moved aside to make room for Ace beside Nina. In his spiffy black tux, paisley waistcoat, and Louis Vuitton, alligator skin, evening wingtips, Ace was turning not only her friend's head his way, but others throughout the ballroom. "You've been avoiding my calls," he whispered confidentially into Nina's ear.

Miffed by his implied intimacy yet unwilling to make a scene, Nina smiled through bared teeth and muttered flatly so no one else could hear, "You know I could have you arrested for stalking."

"Nice shoes," he commented, disregarding her threat. Had he heard her? He tilted his champagne glass toward the Christian Louboutin pumps she'd splurged on for the event.

Without responding, she quickly took her friend's arm and said, for all to hear, "Let's get ourselves some champagne, *si?*" As she steered the surprised woman away, Nina felt someone slip an envelope into her jacket pocket and heard Ace's easily recognizable voice say, "Please open it when you get a chance."

When she did, it was in the taxi on the way home.

There was a ticket and an embossed invitation inside. She'd be mad to throw away a ticket for opening night at the Opera two weeks later, or to turn down the invitation for the exclusive after-party at the Mayor's Sea Cliff home. Nina's dream-come-true, Kiri Te Kanawa, the magical soprano, was going to be there. How did the handsome, disreputable Horace Moon know to hook her through her passion for opera? She cursed the *Chronicle's* photographer who, the season before, captured her in the society page as she came down the Opera House grand stairway after Mozart's *Marriage of Figaro*.

But it was Ace's handwritten list that cinched it for her. List-making, it seemed, they had in common. So too the lined, yellow legal paper he used, exactly like the yellow pads she preferred for her own lists. Nina smiled, recalling how Raul, only the day before, called her out on the habit, accusing her of being a "list-o-maniac" as he systematically crumpled sheets of her outdated yellow lists that regularly cluttered their kitchen table. Nina had argued Raul down to "list-o-phile."

She reread Ace's list many times after that evening. Each time, its presumptuousness, candor, and sincerity made her laugh and warm to him. The list, titled "Ground Rules," had six items—seven, if you counted the indented one.

Ground Rules

1. *Discrete. I won't tell, until you want it known we're dating.*
2. *In public we arrive and leave separately, always surprised to run into one another. Don't worry. It's okay to appear to rebuff me. My skin's thick.*
3. *Promises and truth matter. Ask anyone, especially competitors and detractors—I keep my promises and tell the truth. I will never go behind your back. I hope you won't go behind mine.*
4. *My business and yours are strictly off limits— meaning, no sneaking around, dropping hints, subtle inducements, power games, etc., to get information about what goes on in your office or mine.*

   The Chula lot Tax Sale is off-limits. Period.
5. *I don't believe in "going Dutch." Up front, so it'll never be taken as a bribe—I pick up the tab, always. That's the deal. Except when you cook me dinner, someday.*
6. *You won't be bored. I promise.*

True to his word, he didn't glom onto her that first extraordinary evening. In fact, they hardly spoke. Her ticket in the Opera House was center-Orchestra. She spotted Ace in a box seat high above, but didn't see him close-up until the Mayor's afterparty. Only there, in the throng of San Francisco's "who's who," she did manage a whispered "thank you" before everyone was called to an exquisitely appointed dining room overlooking the Pacific Ocean.

She found her name at a place setting on the opposite side of the table from Ace, but conversation was blocked by a large autumn floral display of goldenrod and eucalyptus. Seated between one of her favorite judges and a young man who regaled her with gripping stories about a harrowing solo sailing adventure to Hawaii, Nina luxuriated in every moment. When Kiri Te Kanawa, dressed in a fairytale gossamer gown, stood to speak, Nina felt the star's brilliant smile beaming straight at her. In that instant, Nina knew the nearness of heaven.

Ace's next communication was discrete, as promised. The note was sent by courier to her office in an envelope marked "personal" with no return address. His message was brief, jotted on yellow lined paper, in list form:

Muir Woods next Saturday?
Logistics, TBA.
415-966-1806

Nina phoned him straight away. He'd earned a walk in the woods, at the least, in thanks for her magical evening. The timing couldn't have been more perfect. Raul was staying with Marty and Amy that weekend, so she had Sunday free. They agreed to meet at the Verdi statue in Golden Gate Park near the Music Concourse. Sufficiently out of the way, it felt unlikely they'd be seen by anyone she knew.

It was ages since Nina had gotten out of the city, and as guarded as she felt about spending the whole day with Ace, she was looking forward to a few hours' respite from the mound of case files waiting for her at home. Knowing well the Bay Area's temperature swings, she'd dressed in layers and packed an extra fleece in her knapsack for the inevitable chill. For shoes, she'd chosen comfort over style: a well-worn pair of tan Nike Air Pliants.

Ace was waiting in his car at their rendezvous statue when Nina's taxi dropped her off. Everything started easily enough. They laughed at the naked bronze cherubs and other figures the sculptor had posed hoisting a flag heroically at the base of the statue. Verdi's bust looked into the distance with amused tolerance for the frenzied drama below.

In his car, Nina found herself following every word as Ace described the silent workings of the shiny, red Honda Insight, an electric and gas combo. It wasn't long, however, before their first argument began. Nina told Ace to take a right turn onto Martin Luther King Drive, the quickest way out of the park to the Golden Gate Bridge, she thought. He said nothing, but grinned as he tore off to the left on a detour into the park.

"Perfect," Nina muttered and settled into the seat, hoping to signal her disapproval in sullen muteness for the remainder of their trip. It didn't last. She was forced to counter him verbally when Ace started a rant about the de Young Museum's redesign as they passed the crumbling old building.

"Why in God's name did we have to go all the way to Switzerland to get a couple of expensive architects, when all the building needed was a bit of shoring up? Have you seen drawings of the monstrosity they're planning?"

"What? You don't like change?" she interrupted. "They're going to great lengths to preserve the feel of the place."

"Fine. Small concession," he retorted sarcastically. "My kids will get to play on the sphinxes, great."

"You have kids?" Nina immediately regretted the personal nature of her question and the implication that it might signify interest in his availability.

"No kids. Not yet," answered Ace, batting his eyes at her with that grin, again.

Somehow, he was able to twist a bit of facial skin and manipulate his mouth to convey innocence, bona fide good humor, and more than a hint of lasciviousness. Despite her better judgment (*did I ever have good judgment when it came to men?* she asked herself), Nina felt drawn into the seductive danger of push-pull emotions. She folded her arms tighter across her middle, mentally preparing her brief:

1. issues,

2. facts of the matter,

3. arguments in support of her position.

"But don't change the subject," Ace barked before she could utter a word. "And don't say I don't like change. I love change, but not when it's going to wreck an iconic beauty, cost a lot of money unnecessarily, and end up with an *arte moderna* deformity."

And so it went, hours flying by with quick, funny, smart, inconsequential banter. They sparred about whether Elin Gonzalez should have been returned to Cuba, though they agreed the embargo made no sense. They also agreed Gore would have been a better president, but disagreed about whether the Florida recount was rigged. The jury remained out after a battle about whether Eminem's lyrics were on a par with Springsteen's *American Skin*. Nina let loose a vehement challenge to Ace's assertion that the internet would change life as they knew it and he accused her of living in a fantasy if she thought the dot-com bubble was about to burst. She said Clinton was an idiot for saddling the US with a trade agreement with China. He said global free trade was the way of the future.

In conclusion, the whole day added up to Nina's idea of a fabulous time. The sky was bright blue, the forest deep and quiet, the sea at Muir Beach sparkling, and the wind a mere whisper behind the makeshift driftwood barrier that Ace found for them, where he spread his picnic delicacies on a thick plaid blanket. Every moment was grand. Only the oncoming fog convinced them to return to the city, where...

"Mom? Everything okay in there?" Raul's question startled Nina from her reverie. The dishes, long done, dried in the rack. *How long had the water been running from the sink faucet?* she wondered.

"I'll be there in a moment," she called back to the dining room. "Sorry. I must have fallen asleep."

When Nina returned to the table, she thanked Marty and Amy for another delicious meal. Marty asked if she should get some horizontal shuteye and give the garden meeting a miss this one time.

She laughed, saying, "Not to fear. I'll sleep very well in the meeting."

MR. ADAMS

Mr. Adams felt content and well fed when he left Lotte's loft and headed a block away to Holy Innocents, the church where the garden committee would meet. Was he imagining that Lotte was more open, friendlier, and more relaxed than he'd noticed before? He sighed, daring to hope that he stood a chance of finding his way into her heart, all the while aware of a higher hurdle: trusting his own heart to open to hers.

The idea of a relationship was daunting. It had been years since he'd felt the frisson of—what could he even call it? Romance? He'd always figured part of him died in the accident, the lasting damage from the trauma. But now…surprise would be an understatement to describe the sensations he felt when Lotte was around. Or how often she walked into his dreams.

Amazing, he mused, shaking his head in disbelief and grateful for the cool night air to clear his thoughts for the meeting ahead.

As he opened the church basement door, he remembered the large sack of cover crop seed he intended to distribute to gardeners to enrich the soil. He could see the mix of oats, cowpeas, and soybeans on his kitchen counter. Ah well, it could wait. He'd give out the seed next time he was in the garden, and at the same time he'd be able to show people how thickly they might broadcast it in their beds for greatest effect.

More importantly however, was ensuring that Jake stayed off the radar of suspicion that evening. Mr. Adams hadn't had a chance to connect with the kid earlier, but he suspected Jake was behind the "banditry." He was less concerned about the damage to the garden than what twisted misery might have provoked Jake to do such a thing. All physical breakage could be repaired with a little effort, and he intended to make sure Jake was involved in the repairs, especially if the damage turned out to come from his handiwork.

He needed first to confirm Jake's role, if any. Mr. Adams knew from experience with troubled students that the last thing the poor kid needed was to be falsely accused. The best Mr. Adams could do for Jake was to stand by him, no matter what. He'd come to like the boy.

True to his cousin Robin's word, Jake completed his community service by helping Mr. Adams in the garden that summer. And after his obligatory hours, Jake continued to show up, always with the same tough-guy look of menace and wearing those ridiculously huge jackboots. But Mr. Adams had come to depend on Jake. Together, they moved wheelbarrows of debris to a Dumpster and dug in a mountain of compost to improve the perimeter beds. On his own, without being asked, Jake picked up the trash that daily blew into the garden. It tickled Mr. Adams to see the kid grin finally when Allegra started calling him Zorro, a name fitting the benevolent outlaw he aspired to be.

So, that morning in the garden, the inconspicuous "Z" punctuating the stage's new graffiti was a telltale giveaway for Mr. Adams...

From down the church hallway, he heard Mrs. Hatfield's "Yoo-hoo!" and restrained his apprehension about Jake with a wave. Her grandson, Neilson, stood beside her.

Beckoning him, she explained, "We're in here. In the Sunday School room. Another group's in our usual room."

Mr. Adams chuckled when he entered the church's kindergarten classroom. A half-dozen giants sat in a circle of tiny chairs. Disproportionately large, everyone's legs sprawled out or bent at gawky angles. They looked like overgrown children. Only Nina's petite, compact frame seemed to fit. He noticed Neilson bringing a larger chair for Mrs. Hatfield through the door, and thought about doing the same for himself. But good-naturedly, if precariously, Mr. Adams bent a long way down into an empty chair.

He may have been the only good-natured person there. By the time he called the meeting to order, 19 neighbors were present, all ready to offer their two cents about what happened in the garden the night before and their advice on what to do about it. Mr. Adams found the tenor of people's feelings alarming. He sensed fear in their anger, and nothing he or anybody else said seemed to assure people. Accusations swirled. Someone said it was the "kids on the corner," and another shouted back, "No way! Those are my kids you're talking about."

Consistent with Allegra's report, Henry lobbied "to bring in the cops to lock up the goddamned crack addicts," and was successful in mobilizing interest in a fence. Its imaginary height loomed large, chained link growing to six feet and aiming higher. Mr. Adams couldn't think of a worse prospect. Its ugly aesthetics aside, a high chain-link fence was not at all the message of hope he wanted the garden to convey for the neighborhood.

He was dismayed to see that two of the people most in support of Henry's proposal were the same complainers who'd individually come to him the week before and asked him to look into the legality of Henry's sculpture. One was Nate, who'd been after Henry's case for months. The other was Millie Peterson, who was the mother of three unruly children. She worried they'd hurt themselves on Henry's sculpture when she wasn't looking—*which was far too often*. The way her children threw their bodies at the sculpture as though it were their own personal jungle gym was only the beginning of a recipe for disaster. Mr. Adams suspected Nate and Millie had consulted one another prior to talking with him, because they each used the specific language of "an attractive nuisance" to refer to the sculpture. Never having heard the term before, Mr. Adams found himself intrigued by the combination of words, but hadn't done a thing to follow up on their requests. Had no plan to, in fact. Here they were now, buddying-up with Henry, the fellow they most criticized. Mr. Adams was dumbfounded to hear Nate tell the group they needed a fence to protect the garden's "infrastructure," and proceeded to list, among other things, Henry's sculpture as one of their most cherished and vulnerable items.

Mr. Adams was grateful for the stalwarts who argued forcefully against a fence. Nina gave a passionate plea for the group to consider how a fence "is a vicious symbol of exclusion that will only invite more trouble from people who feel themselves locked out of the garden." Mr. Adams imagined she must be terrific in the courtroom on behalf of her clients. But he became all the more disheartened when her reasoning only fanned the vehemence of the other side.

A half hour into the mayhem, Mr. Adams was exhausted. The meeting was out of control. He was particularly discouraged when the argument expanded with some neighbors going so far as to call the vandalism a terrorist attack. At least so far no one had accused Jake, and for that he took some comfort. The accusation of terrorism seemed too far out to be credible, but it sealed his decision not to mention anything about working with Jake to make amends. They'd eat the kid alive.

Mostly he felt dragged down by his habitual resistance to conflict. How he regretted that he ever agreed to chair the planning committee. *I hate this kind of thing and I'm lousy at it,* he disparaged. Old, well-trod doubts resurfaced. He wondered whether he could lead the group to a resolution at all, let alone one he could live with. Biting his lip to push these thoughts aside, he tried to direct his attention to the voices volleying in around him. As a last-ditch effort, and feeling more than a little foolish, he recalled the conversation with Lotte and Allegra and silently asked for assistance from the garden.

Mr. Adams would later wonder if what happened next was due to coincidence or the garden's blessing. Whichever, when Josie raised her hand, her timing was impeccable. Mr. Adams asked for quiet so she could speak. Miraculously the room went quiet for the first time.

Josie stood. Though towering above the ring of little chairs, there was nothing intimidating about her stance. Her shoulders hunched and she clasped her hands in front of her. It was the first time Mr. Adams had ever seen Josie in pants, or looking disheveled. Her blue jeans were faded and torn at the knees. A worn sweatshirt hung limp on her slender frame. Heavy circles shadowed her eyes. Her gaunt cheeks, darkened by a day's beard growth, gave lie to her chosen gender. Her red high-top sneakers and gaudy headscarf, once hallmarks of her outrageous playfulness, seemed incongruous tonight and accentuated the fact something was very wrong.

"I didn't want to come," she murmured, her faint voice barely audible. "But Paulo begged me." She faltered and drew her hand slowly down over her face, as if trying to re-mask. "He's dying…maybe tonight. Maybe tomorrow." Mr. Adams watched helplessly as Josie pressed her fists into her hips and took a deep breath. "He wanted me to tell you he loves the garden. It's the thing he was most proud of doing in his life... of anything else, anywhere."

Mr. Adams heard Millie's muted gasp from across the room. She was crying. Mrs. Hatfield was also in tears. She brought an embroidered handkerchief from her purse and put her hand to her heart. Next to her, Neilson looked down and shuffled his feet under the chair.

Josie stood unmoving, her voice barely audible. "He wanted me to tell you 'thank you'...for letting him belong to you..." Mr. Adams felt Josie's gentle eyes upon him as she moved her tender gaze to each person in the circle. "Thank you, and you, and...all of us." Wiping the arm of her sweatshirt across her face, Josie continued, her voice seeming to Mr. Adams to gain strength. "Paulo wanted to tell you that...the garden thanks you too. And..." Josie swallowed deeply. "... It loves us...all. He said we have to remember this. Always." Then, with a wan smile, Josie spread her hands broadly. "You know Paulo...always Mr. Dramatic. He wants...he wants us to spread his ashes in the garden and have a party...on *Dia de los Muertos*, when else? Halloween...costumes, the works..."

Seeing Josie's thin shoulders heave with quiet weeping, Mr. Adams stood and walked around to stand behind her, his own cheeks glistening with tears. He opened his arms and drew Josie into a warm embrace. "Go home to Paulo. Give him our love. Tell him it's all set for Halloween."

Mr. Adams held her until Josie turned to the group. She waved a tired farewell.

Mr. Adams spoke to the hushed circle of friends, "Like Paolo, I'm grateful to all of you too, and to the garden. Mrs. Hatfield has graciously brought us cookies, I see, and the tea water's hot."

Before others stood up Nina said, "My kid and I will be in the garden tomorrow to help clean up."

Henry nodded and said, "Me too."

LIZ

It was past midnight when Liz's taxi pulled up across from the garden. Home from work. The street was dark and still. A heavy fog had settled thick onto the street, muffling the faraway sounds of traffic and dimming the glow of streetlamps. Only a few lights remained on in her building, and she was pleased to see one was Lotte's. As was often the case, Liz was still buzzing after finishing a last set at the restaurant. She hoped Lotte would be up for a cup of tea—and, tonight, some consolation.

Liz knocked lightly and cracked open Lotte's door and when she saw Lotte sitting on her meditation cushion. She whispered, "I don't want to interrupt."

But Lotte stood and beckoned for her to join her. "Come, sit next to me on the couch. I was working late on the book and am still awake, though barely."

Liz stepped in and motioned to Lotte that she'd first peek in on Allegra. She blew her sleeping child a kiss, then shut the bedroom door quietly and headed into the kitchen. "I need some chamomile. You?"

"I'm good," answered Lotte as she curled under a cozy blanket on the couch.

Soon, her mug filled with steaming tea in hand, Liz eased onto the opposite end of the couch and tucked her feet under Lotte's blanket. She felt herself relax for the first time since that horrid phone call from Anna. She relished the comfortable silence between Lotte and herself and wondered if she'd spoil it by talking about the call.

Liz appreciated how Lotte could hold silence, as if there were all the time in the world to speak or do anything else. Liz, on the other hand, was aware of her own limitations in comparison. Most of the time she met each moment with impatience to get onto the next and on to the other side, and then stepping back, fearful of what the other side might hold. She found herself trying to formulate how she would talk about the phone call with Anna when she realized how exhausted Lotte looked.

"Hey. You okay? You look completely done-in."

"Well, it is past midnight."

Although Lotte smiled when she said this, Liz sensed something else must be wrong. Could she have heard about Anna? *Likely not,* she thought as Lotte continued.

"It's been a full day...very up and down." Lotte pursed her lips. "And the material that's turning up in my research for the book about lies is so disturbing. It's hard to read. Brings up stuff I thought I'd dealt with safely and tucked away." Liz saw Lotte shudder, then tuck the blanket up tightly around her as she fixed her gaze on a distant point in the ceiling. Before Liz could think how to respond, Lotte shrugged and continued, "If I believed in astrology, I'd bet planets are crashing. By now, you've gotten wind of what happened in the garden?"

Liz heard Lotte sigh deeply and knew something bad must have taken place. But when Lotte described events at the garden, how someone had tipped over the worm bin and painted graffiti on the stage, Liz was relieved to hear the news was not as worrisome as Lotte's concerned look gave her to fear. It seemed everything could be easily fixed with a little elbow grease.

"I haven't seen it myself," said Lotte, "but John and Allegra..."

The name John stumped Liz for only a moment. "John, is it?" she teased, and grinned when Lotte rolled her eyes.

Not really wanting to embarrass Lotte, Liz returned

to the garden and asked how Allegra was taking it all. She was glad to hear Allegra was more excited than upset, especially because some of her worm friends chose to stick around in the toppled bin.

"Well, she sings to them every day, and sets aside a worms' ration at every meal. I'd hope they'd show some loyalty," laughed Liz.

"That's what John said, too. He stayed for dinner."

"Right…?" Liz wondered where Lotte was taking them with this new turn in the conversation, not that it mattered nor was all that surprising. She'd been entertained for months by the slow, tentative unfolding of their romance, even if they themselves seemed oblivious to what was happening. In fact, everyone in the garden was rooting for them on the sidelines. She'd heard rumors of bets being taken. For the moment though, Liz was grateful for whatever diversion drew her away from her own personal melodrama. She smiled coyly at Lotte and bunched a pillow behind her head, settling into the couch.

"You with your innuendos," said Lotte. "You're as bad as Allegra. She's a shameless matchmaker, not in the least subtle. If she wasn't so cute, I'd—"

"Trust her, Lotte," advised Liz, with confidence. "She never liked any of my boyfriends, with good reason. He's a kind and caring person, and he likes you. A lot. You can see that."

"Hmmm...I admit I am leaning closer to it," said Lotte. When Liz responded wide-eyed in mock disbelief, Lotte repeated, "I am. Don't look so surprised. Though, maybe I'm only getting a micro-millimeter closer at a time..."

They sat in silence then until Liz, hating to interrupt the moment's sweetness by introducing her own troubles into the conversation, pressed ahead anyway. It seemed as good a time as any, and she was loath to go to bed without Lotte's support.

"Lotte, I'm glad things are getting sorted out for you, but I'm kind of a wreck again." With words spilling out, memories of the day's rush of confusion, raw fury, and guilt flooded in. Liz kicked petulantly against the couch cushion under the blanket, and then reddened, mortified by her childish behavior in the face of Lotte's serenity.

"It would be hard not to feel that way," Lotte commented. "I saw Vince today and he told me some of it."

"That asshole," exploded Liz at the mention of her father. Despite her resolve to stay calm she had rushed to judge—but he deserved it, and more. She interpreted the slight movement of Lotte's brow as disapproval of her name-calling and propelled herself off the couch in defense. "What else do you call someone like that? Not only does he screw his students, this one he knocks up while married to my mom! My poor mother. Jesus."

Lotte's nonresponse made Liz feel all the more ragged, messy, and out of control. She yelled, "Enough with the silence and lifted eyebrow. Dammit, say something, will you?"

"Getting angry with me won't help."

"I know. I know," apologized Liz, trying to rein in her emotions by breathing in a long inhalation and letting it out before continuing. "I'm sorry. But it's all so fucking messed up. It makes me crazy." She flopped back again on the couch opposite Lotte and grabbed the pillow to her chest.

"Going crazy I can understand," said Lotte. "I went crazy myself, if you recall. Hmmm...with that very same man, your father, and for not dissimilar reasons. I tasted my resentment again this afternoon when he told me about Anna. But tonight..."

Liz sensed Lotte grew taller, and stronger. She noted a slight rise on her breast from her breath, the older woman's only movement until Lotte broke the silence between them. "Hmmm...tonight, I understand that he's a desperate man. A desperately frightened man. Back then, and probably still now."

This seemed ludicrous to Liz, and way off the mark. Her laugh was immediate, impatient, and harsh. "You must be kidding. That bastard? Frightened of what?"

"Of you. Of your mother."

"For God's sake, I was a baby when he was messing around. Him...frightened of a little baby?" exclaimed Liz. In an afterthought, she added, "I don't know how old I was when...but I couldn't have been more than a toddler. This Anna person's—"

"...the same age, or nearly," Lotte interjected.

"Are you shitting me?" shouted Liz, shaking her head in disbelief as the significance of the timing dawned on her. "That means Mom was pregnant! That creepy, horrible, lying, slimebag bastard."

"Liz. Think about it. He must have been terrified."

"Of what?" spat Liz. She threw off the pillow and drew in her knees tightly against her chest, tucked her face between them and squeezed herself into a ball as she'd witnessed Allegra doing when holding back a tantrum.

"Of love...?" Lotte replied, a questioning look on her face.

"You can't be serious," mumbled Liz, sickened that Lotte would feel anything but the same raw anger she felt for her pathetic father. Sickened that Lotte was making excuses for Vince. Liz bit her tongue and tried to shut Lotte's words out as Lotte persisted.

"Tonight...when you looked in on Allegra? What were you feeling?"

She shrugged, not sure where Lotte was going.

She looked up to find Lotte's kindly eyes. "Happy," she answered. "Happy to see her peaceful, lying there. Her little face, all her animals around her. But what's this got to do with anything?"

"What else did you feel?"

To her surprise, tears sprang from Liz's eyes. "I don't know. Gratitude? That…that she's okay, in spite of everything? In spite of me. That she wakes up happy now, these mornings." She hid her face again, hoping to dull the fierce pain of her love for Allegra, mixed with dark regret for the years she wasn't there for her daughter. Liz felt Lotte's hand rest gently on her head and resisted the swift urge to bat it away.

"Sometimes the feelings I have looking at Allegra, and when I watch you too, Liz, are, hmmm…so *tender* that the muscle of my heart literally aches. You know what I mean?"

"Every day," answered Liz, forcing herself to face Lotte. She dried her tears on the cuff of her sweater, determined to remain cool. "Every day."

"I suspect Vince felt the same, and still does now. Only what's tender, however excruciating for us, is for him, terrifying." Lotte's voice changed to a whisper as she shook her head slowly back and forth. "…terrifying in ways you and I can't begin to imagine."

Liz tried to let this sink in. She shifted her weight on the couch, resisting the urge to flee or worse, to strike out at Lotte. She was sick of Lotte's high ground and these feeble attempts to mask the truth of her father's deplorable, narcissistic cruelty. It took all of her concentration to tamp down her temper and allow Lotte to continue.

"I think the only way he knows to deal with his terror of love is to thrash around and find a way to dodge it. Work, other women, booze—they all serve as ways to back off from, to hide from love, so he can feel safe. Safety...isn't that what we all want? Of course, I don't know if any of this is true for Vince. I shouldn't speak for him, but my guess is that it's something like this."

Liz was not in the least persuaded, and felt more angered than comforted. "That's pure bullshit. He wouldn't know the first thing about love."

Lotte interrupted before she could continue. "He may not have loved you the way you wanted to be loved, Liz. But you and Allegra are more precious to him than life itself."

"Well, he's got a sucky way of showing it," barked Liz. Feeling bone-tired, she sighed loudly. It was way past time for heading to her own apartment. As she rose from the couch, she felt Lotte's hand reach out for hers.

"Don't go just yet, Liz. What happened today? On the phone with Anna?"

Liz cringed. *Ah, now she's going for the mark.*

Knowing it would be fruitless to try to duck from Lotte's question, Liz willed herself to stay and let the worst unfold as it may. Failing the courage to face Lotte, she set off for the kitchen, mug in hand, and once there, she washed it clean. She then gripped the side of the counter with both hands.

"No surprise there. I wasn't very nice," she admitted. "Actually, I hung up on her. Really, what would anyone do? I was sitting there in the apartment, going over music scores for tonight and rehearsing octaves when the phone rang. It's a perfect stranger saying, 'Hi, I'm your long-lost sister.'"

Liz wished her recount of the phone call sounded less like a sullen teenager and more like the grown-up she was trying so hard to become. She tried again.

"Well, not like that, really. I don't remember what she said, but I kind of remember what I said. I told her never to call again, or something to that effect, and slammed down the phone. And, yes, you're absolutely right," she admitted, looking at her feet to avoid Lotte's eyes, "I am not proud of the way I handled it."

When Lotte didn't respond, Liz continued, "Then I went numb. When I got to work, Nick said I looked like I was about to heave. Throw it all up, right there in the bar. Somehow, I managed to keep it all in, rather than chucking up on my new dress, and got to the stage. In the middle of my set, I thawed. Something in that Bluesy music I was doing, I guess. I thought I was going to blow it right there. Thank God I pushed the feelings into the song and...well, it worked out okay.

"Nick took me out for coffee afterwards. That man's hardly had a night's sleep since I got out of treatment..." She told Lotte about their AA talk. "Of course, everything's out of control,' I told Nick. 'When you pick up a phone one day and learn you're no longer an only child. How can I trust a higher power when the supposed higher power in a family always proves to be totally out of control, and hurtful?'"

She described how Nick patiently reminded her that she could trust in her AA friends who loved her, and that if she kept away from drink, got to a meeting ASAP, and took it one day at a time, somehow, she would survive this.

"Blah, blah, blah. Why am I so desperate to hear this comforting crap?" Liz heard herself whining. "And here I am, talking it again to death, like an idiot." Liz clamped her arms over her chest, and announced, determined this time, "Look, I should go up to bed."

"Liz, do you think you'll drink over this?"

Liz felt like a horse kicked her in the gut. She hunched over and gagged. When she could, she shot back at Lotte, "What is this? Fucking—are you trying to see what else you can say to puncture my self-esteem, once and for all today?"

Abruptly, she grabbed her jacket off the end of the couch, snatched up her purse, and started for the door. Hand on doorknob, Liz stopped at once when the full force of Lotte's voice hit her.

"Don't you walk out on me."

"What?" burst Liz, her own rage discharging. In an exaggerated whisper, she blasted back at Lotte, mimicking her words, "Don't you raise your voice," and then added sarcastically, "Allegra's sleeping, or don't you remember?"

"How dare you tell me how to act in my own home?"

Stunned, Liz watched Lotte stand, her face threatening in a way that was totally unfamiliar to Liz. She felt herself freeze, unable to move one way or the other.

"Who do you think you are?" Lotte yelled.

Lotte's words startled Liz into motion. She swung open the loft door, and shouted back at Lotte, "And who the hell do you think *you* are? My mother?"

Slamming the door behind her, she stood in the hallway, astonished by what had just happened. She heard Lotte's muffled sobbing behind the door and was overcome by an extreme thirst and dry throat. She recognized the need and knew well how to satisfy it. On her way to the elevator, Liz felt a cold breeze on her face. Someone had left a window open down the hall. She brought a hand to her cheek momentarily, then checked out the time on the thin, gold wrist-watch she wore—a relic of her mother's.

There was still time. There were places open. Tips were good that night at Nick's. She had enough money. One drink wouldn't hurt.

Would it?

Then, surprising herself, she kissed her fingers twice and knew, for the first time in a long time, exactly what she needed to do. She took her key ring out of her coat pocket and slid one of the keys into the lock on Lotte's door. She pulled open the heavy door and walked back inside.

WINTER

WINTER SOLSTICE ROUND

Deep down in the belly of the night
dream deep winter dreams,
and lie safe in your grandmother's arms
still as a seed,
still as a seed.

Becky Reardon. *Follow the Motion* (cd)

ALLEGRA

Allegra woke to the peaceful silence that filled the loft when Lotte was meditating. She brought the comforter up around her chin and snuggled further into the soft warmth. She hoped her Mom, probably still asleep upstairs in their loft, would get up in time to come downstairs for breakfast in Lotte's loft with them. She crossed the first two fingers on her right hand and kissed them twice, sealing a wish that Lotte would make pancakes. Once, Liz showed Allegra how she did this for wishes when she was a little girl. Allegra hoped it worked for pancakes. But to be safe, she rehearsed two good reasons, in case Lotte didn't already have pancakes in mind, why she should. One, it wasn't a school day, and two, it was the night before Christmas. *No*, she corrected, *it's the morning of the night before Christmas.*

Allegra then set about systematically straightening out her stuffed animals that were scattered higgledy-piggledy under the covers after their night's sleep. Each got a kiss as she laid them down with their heads on her pillow. There was Fred, the dog; Eenie, the parakeet; Lump, the elephant; Baby Girl, a gorilla; and Panda, a black-and-white bear. For as long as she could remember, every night before going to sleep, Allegra made sure that her animals were in place, just so. The hardest part was remembering everyone's place. She always was careful to rotate the animals so they wouldn't think she had favorites. This meant moving the animal who lay next to her the night before to the outer edge of the row of other animals. She'd done this in all of her beds—the one in New York, and now her two beds here in San Francisco: the one in Lotte's loft and the one upstairs. Allegra couldn't imagine going to sleep without putting her animals to bed next to her, in order. She hardly ever forgot, but when she did, the animals said it was okay. Actually, they didn't say anything when she did forget, and Allegra wasn't altogether sure it was okay. She suspected they only pretended it was okay she forgot so they didn't hurt her feelings.

A faint tap on the door to her room put a stop to her uneasy thoughts. Her mom's face was peering from behind the door, asking "One-two-three...ready?"

"Oh no!" screamed Allegra, laughing. Worm hugs. She dove under her comforter in time as Liz plopped down on the bed next to her and began squirming and cuddling against her, singing, "Worm hugs! Worm hugs!"

It all started one morning in Liz's bed when Allegra tried to explain to her about seeing worms "may-ting." To demonstrate, she'd plastered her arms against her pajamas and schmushed herself up next to Liz. It was so silly they couldn't stop laughing. From then on, she'd come to expect it every morning.

With Liz pressing in, Allegra wiggled far over to the edge of the bed next to the wall until she felt Liz's body relax her pushing. Allegra started humming in the loud monotone she called "worm music." Liz turned it into a familiar tune and sang the words…

Down by the station
Early in the morning
Hear the puffer-bellies all in a row.

Allegra sang along under the covers, imagining that her muffled voice sounded like a worm under the soil. "Puffer-bellies" was her favorite song when she was a tiny little girl. They hadn't sung it for a long time, and it felt good to hear it again, even if it was a baby song. She and Liz sang through the verses again and again until Allegra came up for air. She pushed the comforter away from her face to find Lotte standing by the bed.

"Any room in there for another worm?" asked Lotte. And before Allegra could answer, Lotte also fell onto the bed and instructed Allegra to squiggle in from her side so they could make a squished worm-club-sandwich with Liz in the middle. Allegra braced her feet against the wall next to her and pushed as hard as she could before giving in to giggles. They were all laughing then—the animals too, scattered every which way again.

Allegra raised her eyebrows at her mom as Lotte untangled from the overflowing bed and raced to the bathroom, shouting, "Lord, will my bladder hold?"

"A good aerobic start for a busy day, right?" asked Liz.

Allegra smiled, feeling happy down to her toes. She admired the smooth white folds of her angel costume, pressed and starched on its hanger across the room. A gold, tinsel halo sparkled as it hung from a peg in the closet, and her gauzy, veined wings got ready to fly off the back of her desk chair.

"Let's see," she heard Liz say, as she ticked through her fingers one by one. "I have my AA meeting at 11 this morning, right? We've got to get to church early, by five o'clock. Remember, Mr. Adams is taking you to the park this morning. He also wants to show you something in the garden."

"We're gonna take the snails to the park," Allegra eagerly explained to her mother. "The kids in the garden have been collecting snails for weeks." She reminded Liz about how they'd already filled four large buckets and how they had to cover them so they wouldn't crawl out. She and Mr. Adams were going to take them to Mission Dolores Park to let them go free so they could find new homes, far from the garden, because they were eating everybody's plants. For every fifty snails each kid put in a bucket, they'd get a present at the Christmas carol singing party that night. It was a cinch to find fifty snails. She already had five presents coming to her.

"Mr. Adams has something else too to show you in the garden. You never know. Could be something special," said Liz, piquing Allegra's curiosity.

Allegra shot up in bed. "What?"

"I'm not going to tell," said Liz. "It's Christmas. All kinds of stuff is possible."

"It's not Christmas yet," corrected Allegra. "Tomorrow's Christmas."

"Right you are. How could I forget?"

Not ready to get up, Allegra watched from bed while her mom chose clothes for her from her chest of drawers. She assured Liz that she'd *already* brought everything down with her the night before: her costume, tights, and party shoes for the pageant. So no, she didn't need anything from upstairs. And yes, she was going to wear her costume to the party that night.

-

Breakfast was the best. Pancakes *and* Mr. Adams. He came in while Allegra was setting the table. She hoped he'd sit next to her, but before she could even ask, he said he wanted to sit next to Lotte. So he sat between both of them, and Liz had to sit on the other side.

"At a round table there are no sides," Lotte told her, and Allegra spent some time thinking about this as she ate her pancakes. Then Liz interrupted her thoughts by asking her to recite her lines for church that evening.

She gladly stood up and bowed. "Okay. First I point to where the Baby Hey-zeus is, and then I say, 'Mira! Esta un nee-n-yo, el ee-ho de Dee-os!' It's Spanish." When Lotte and Liz clapped, Allegra clapped too and twirled around two times on her tippy-toes.

Mr. Adams exclaimed, "Brava!"

Allegra explained how Mimi, another angel, was going to follow with the same thing in English. "She says 'Look, it's a boy, the son of God!'"

When Liz asked if she was nervous, Allegra said, "No," and she wasn't a bit. "I want another pancake."

After breakfast, Liz left, and Lotte and Mr. Adams sat and talked while Allegra worked on the brightly colored jigsaw puzzle she'd started the night before, a pretty picture of kids at the beach. Eager to see what Mr. Adams's surprise was, she kept interrupting their talking to ask him to take her to the garden. Each time, he laughed, and they kept talking.

"You two could talk all day long!"

They agreed she was probably right, but didn't stop talking. She thought they'd never finish. Finally, Mr. Adams said he didn't want another cup of tea. One whole side of her puzzle was done by then, revealing a pail and shovel and a big whale and her baby whale, both made of sand. Mr. Adams stood up from the table and asked Allegra, "What are you waiting for? Let's go."

"Me?" shouted Allegra. Carefully, she slid the puzzle under the chair so it wouldn't get hurt, jumped up, and raced to get her jacket from the hook by the door. Holding the door open, she asked Mr. Adams, "What are you waiting for?" Once in the hallway, the two didn't bother waiting for the slow, squeaky elevator; instead, Allegra skipped down the three flights of stairs with Mr. Adams following behind.

It was chilly outside. Allegra zippered her purple fleece up to her neck, looked up into the gray sky, and thought how lucky it was that they beat the rain. Across the street, the garden looked cold and dark. There were no kids or anybody else in the garden that morning. She wondered if anyone would come out at all.

"Henry's fence is lonely," she observed aloud.

It was the craziest fence she'd ever seen—more like a jungle gym. That's because of all the work that Henry and Jake had done fixing it. She was really annoyed that Henry let Jake help build it and not her. Jake got to wear the Darth Vader helmet that Henry wore when using the welding torch, but he never once asked her if she wanted to try it on. It made her mad she had to watch from far-off as they aimed the hissing blue flame on Henry's sculpture, which the bandits had pushed over and was now a fence.

She watched them take the whole sculpture apart. Then they re-attached everything, but running sideways. What used to go up now spread along two sides of the garden. Weird pieces of thing-a-ma-jigs went this way and fit in that way so kids could crawl in and out and over. She loved to ride the pale pink carousel horses for hours with her friends. In one place, you could scoot down and duck-waddle through the hollow of a worm belly made out of a stiff plastic tube, curled around like a huge Slinky, round and round.

Allegra wondered if people would sing carols in the garden in the rain. Like he knew what she was thinking, Mr. Adams said, "I expect we'll be up in Lotte's loft this evening. The weather won't hold much longer."

Allegra darted into the garden through Mr. Adams's archway. With Henry's fence around the garden, everyone went into the garden under the arch these days, except if they wanted to come through on the alley side by the stage where there was no fence yet. She called back to Mr. Adams, "Hurry! Where's my surprise?"

Then she saw it. Allegra clapped her hands to her cheeks in amazement. Across the garden, in the wildflower patch next to the worm box, was the sweetest little house she ever saw. Its steep roof, shingles, and curlicue carvings looked something like a cross between the gingerbread house she and Liz recently baked and the witch house that Hansel and Gretel found in the woods. Only this house was on long legs, nearly as high off the ground as she was tall. She looked back at slowpoke Mr. Adams, hoping to hurry him along.

"What is it?"

Wordlessly he smiled, so she ran ahead without him. When she got nearer, she was surprised to see Jake kneeling under the house.

"What are you doing here?" she asked.

But then, of course he'd be there, she remembered. He'd promised to show her where there was a huge bunch of snails.

"Do you like it? See, this screen on the porch. I helped Mr. A. make it," said Jake.

Allegra stuck her tongue out at him because he was a bragger, something a boy in her class once called her when she told him she was best in science.

Feeling like a huge Alice in Wonderland, she pulled on a tiny front doorknob, but it didn't open. So, she walked around the house where she saw a padlock in one corner. The lock wouldn't budge when she pulled on it. It wanted a key.

"Who lives here?" Allegra impatiently asked Mr. Adams as he joined them and shook hands with Jake.

"You'll know soon," was Mr. Adams's mysterious response. "Let's see if someone's home."

He took a big keyring from his pocket and detached a tiny key that fit perfectly into the padlock. Allegra stepped aside as, with the click of the key, the whole back wall of the house swung out in front of her

Allegra looked inside. "Anyone home?"

She felt the warmth and quiet of the house as soon as she peeked into its one large room. The loose hay was dotted with tiny, round, black balls, bigger than the silver balls on cupcakes. In the room's dim light Allegra saw two gray heaps huddled in one corner.

"Oooooh...so cute," she cooed. "Baby bunnies! Can I touch one?" she begged Jake as he reached into the room and gently cradled one of the rabbits in his hands.

"Sit down—the bunny will feel safe in your lap," he told her.

Allegra sat on one of the upturned buckets nearby and cupped her hands on her lap. Breathlessly, she watched Jake close the wall of the house with his hip, then kneel beside her and place the rabbit in her hands. It squirmed in her hands, then pressed its back feet into her thighs. At first, she was afraid it would jump, so she quickly closed her hands around its body as tenderly as she could, then remained still. Before long, the rabbit snuggled into the stillness with only a twitch of its lips.

"Will he bite?" she asked softly, frightened to move.

"Not likely," answered Mr. Adams as he settled into the bucket next to her. "I think she likes being held. Both were raised by a large family, and they're pretty used to being with children. They probably miss their old friends."

"Awwww, poor babies," sympathized Allegra as she patted the tiny furry head lightly with her first two fingers. "That's okay. I'll be your friend," she said to comfort the small creature. "Is it a he or a she?"

"They're both females," answered Mr. Adams. "Sisters."

"Two sisters," echoed Allegra. Her confidence growing, she stroked the rabbit's soft ears and the fur down its back, feeling the thin bones underneath. Allegra was enthralled by the sensation of a tiny heartbeat racing under her hands. "What should I call them?"

Jake answered, "They used to be 'Granny' and 'Godzilla.' But they won't mind if you give them new names."

"Oh no," disagreed Allegra, thinking Jake was mean to even suggest such a thing. "I wouldn't do that. Is this Granny or Godzilla?"

"...I don't know."

"Are you Granny?" The rabbit stayed perfectly still except for twitching lips and nose as Allegra bent down and looked it in the eye. "Granny?" When the rabbit didn't respond, Allegra sat up and declared it must be Godzilla. Mr. Adams agreed, it must be Godzilla.

Allegra asked Jake to get Granny to join her sister. He reached into the house and placed Granny in her lap as he took Godzilla.

"See," observed Allegra, touching the rabbit's head, "You can tell this is Granny because she has a white spot here on her head, like the one Lotte has where her hair is turning white."

Mr. Adams laughed, and after a while he said they should put the rabbits back on the hay-covered floor so he and Jake could give Allegra a tour of the house. Jake showed her where to put food and water and how to open the roof on hot days. He explained how the porch floor was part wood slats and part screen so rain wouldn't puddle, and so the rabbits' poop would drop down to the ground below.

Jake was beginning to make Allegra cross. He was acting like such a know-it-all. She wasn't happy about having to share the rabbits with him. Then she changed her mind, as she sometimes did, and decided it was okay—even though Raul called Jake a "weirdo punk." She and Jake were friends since he told her a secret she promised never to tell: that his father was dead, like hers was too.

Her attention returned to Granny and Godzilla as Mr. Adams explained how the legs—he called them *stilts*—that were holding up the house were set in concrete so it couldn't topple over, and that the metal cones on each leg prevented snakes and mice from sharing the rabbits' food. The idea that snakes might invade the rabbit house made Allegra's skin crawl.

"Don't worry, Godzilla and Granny," she whispered to soothe the rabbits, in case they were frightened hearing about it. The rabbits seemed okay. When Mr. Adams moved on to explain how to dump the straw out to clean the house, Allegra was all for cleaning the house then and there. She pouted when he told her it wasn't dirty yet because Jake put new bedding in only the night before.

Curiosity bumped aside her grumpiness as she watched Mr. Adams sift through some of the straw with his fingers and found several of the little black balls she'd seen before.

"This is rabbit poop," he said, holding his hand so Allegra could see. "Worms love it. They think it's candy, and it makes terrific compost, too."

"Uuuugh," said Allegra, holding her nose, not caring for the worms' taste in candy. She knew that this was sure not something she would want to put on frosting. But when Jake opened the lid of the worm box and tossed in a handful, Allegra clapped her hands and hummed a rousing version of "O Come, All Ye Faithful," and Mr. Adams joined in.

Once the caroling was over, Mr. Adams reminded them of their snail duties. "I think we'll be able to get to the park before it rains," he said, showing her how to close the padlock on the rabbit house so her new friends would be safe.

"Bye Granny. Bye Godzilla. I'll be back soon," she promised and blew two loud kisses at the little house before picking up one of the snail buckets.

She reached for Mr. Adams's jacket pocket with her free hand and together, all three of them set off. Mr. Adams topped off everything when he said, "And afterward, if there's time, I want to go to The Flying Saucer for a fancy Christmas Eve—lunch if that's okay with you and Jake?"

Wow, that was her favorite restaurant. Allegra thought it was a really good plan. She could already taste her black bean and banana pie.

MR. ADAMS

"I turned around and they were gone." Rain-drenched and chilled, Mr. Adams stood in Lotte's doorway, conscious of nothing but the panic in her face and his wish that this wasn't happening. He explained that the downpour started as they reached the park. He'd dumped the sticky snails from his buckets under a nearby hedge as quickly as possible, expecting the children to do the same with their buckets. But the next moment, they were nowhere in sight. "I retraced our route. They're not here, are they? They're probably in the garden and I must have missed them."

"What are you saying? Allegra's not with you? Are you serious?" Lotte's rapid-fire questions fell like barbs, leaving Mr. Adams reeling in confusion about what next to say or do. He was impressed and alarmed

by how quickly Lotte flew into action—grabbing her keys, she threw open the loft door. He reached for her coat on the peg by the wall.

"Forget about that!" she shouted.

Mr. Adams hurriedly draped the coat over his arm despite Lotte's refusal to wear it and followed as speedily as he could down the stairs. He didn't catch up with Lotte, nor could he catch his breath sufficiently to respond to the trailing barrage of questions flying back at him up the stairwell.

"Did you call the police? When did you last see her? Did you check the garden yet? How could you let her out of your sight?"

Any momentary relief he felt as Lotte waited for him on the sidewalk was replaced by fear that he had disappointed her beyond repair—or worse, that she would no longer trust him to care for Allegra. He took the full force of Lotte's anger. She stopped short of calling him irresponsible, but her words carried unnerving venom. Though he recognized that her anger masked her understandable fears, he was peeved that she would blast at him this way when, as a team, they needed to be focused on finding the children. He knew enough to keep that thought to himself.

"Look," he said instead, hoping to reassure her. "They're okay. They're somewhere near and we'll find them soon. Allegra's not alone. She's with Jake." He

placed Lotte's coat over her already wet shoulders and held his breath as he heard the hiss of her in-drawn breath.

He caught the look of dread in the glance of her dark, moist eyes, and in her whispered question: "John, she's with that boy?"

"Jake," he answered, trying to reassure her. "He's not the 'that boy' you think he is. I trust him, as does Allegra."

In Lotte's sharp glance Mr. Adams read that this wasn't the time for him to convey his conviction of the boy's goodness, witnessed over countless hours with Jake by his side in the garden. Although Jake's demeanor remained desultory on the outside and his words often rubbed people the wrong way, he'd grown on Mr. Adams. Underneath Jake's surly exterior, Mr. Adams recognized an eagerness to please and a willingness to lend a hand…if approached obliquely, without triggering Jake's rebel-without-a-cause reflex. Most recently, Mr. Adams had been impressed by Jake's ingenuity with some of the trickier carpentry involved in making the rabbit hutch. Henry would vouch the same. An unlikely pair, cantankerous Henry and taciturn Jake had worked together for days on the heavy lifting and painstaking welding required for the garden's new fence. Moreover, the fact that Jake had Allegra's trust was no small measure of the boy's character.

This wasn't the time to explain anything. Instead, Mr. Adams simply held out his hand for her to take.

"Hmmm...Well, we'll see, won't we?" was her chilling response as she rejected his hand.

Mr. Adams cursed himself. He should at least know Jake's address. The boy's parents' names? He didn't even have the address for Robin, Jake's cousin and Mr. Adams's former student who'd prevailed on him to take in the boy in the first place. From their first days together, Mr. Adams sensed a nervousness in Jake whenever he was asked anything of a personal nature. So, Mr. Adams naturally steered clear, knowing it would only be time before Jake opened up on his own. He'd found it was often like this with the kids who found their way to his janitor's basement sanctuary at school. When they first arrived, especially the shy, sullen types, they were unforthcoming to the point of antisocial. Then one day, for no particular reason other than the passage of time, they'd spill their guts and share deep secrets, shame, and grief. No direct questions and first names only—these were the unwritten rules between the basement kids and Mr. Adams. It suited him fine. In his workspace, teens could experience at least a moment's respite from the constant crosscurrents of their peers' judgements and adults' expectations in the school hallways above and at home.

Now in the face of Lotte's tacit condemnation, his wish not to alienate the secretive Jake by probing for personal information seemed a frail excuse. Lotte was right to think him daft. Mr. Adams stumbled and caught his step as he navigated around a puddle in the middle of the street. Lotte reached the garden first and he watched her rush in the direction of the rabbit hutch. He shoved freezing fingers into the pockets of his worn woolen jacket and began calling the children's names, echoing Lotte's cries from the other side of the garden.

Nearing the deserted stage, Mr. Adams heard a rustling noise. Sure enough, Jake was crawling out from under the back corner. "Everything's cool, Mr. A."

"Everything is most certainly *not* cool, young man," shouted Lotte as she careened past Mr. Adams to Allegra, who was standing beside Jake by then. Lotte swooped Allegra into her arms. "Oh, baby..."

"Don't cry, Lotte," wailed Allegra. "Please. Please don't cry."

Absurdly, Mr. Adams wished he could join the circle of their arms and comfort them both, and be comforted himself. But Lotte's tight embrace of this dear child, now safe and sound, held no room for him. He turned to face Jake.

"I fucked up, didn't I, Mr. A.?"

sauerkraut's our meat menu today, with a side of fresh dug Yukon potatoes swimming in a mustard sauce with parsley and Wright's Dairy butter. That's it for our specials, but we can make pretty much any version of a happy hen egg omelet or garden green salad you can imagine. Let me know. I'll bring water and a basket of rolls fresh out of the oven while you decide."

-

After lunch, Lotte and Allegra left Mr. Adams with Jake in the garden. He could tell by her unusually quiet manner at the restaurant that Lotte was still miffed with him. Given that Jake was more than his usual, sultry self, Mr. Adams was happy they managed to keep the conversation going at all. He credited Allegra's effervescence entirely.

"Jake," he asked when they were alone. "Take me to where you live. I need to meet your family." Mr. Adams watched the boy shrink before him.

"Not a good idea, Mr. A." Jake fidgeted with the ties on his sweatshirt.

Leaning in to catch Jake's eye, Mr. Adams spoke softly so as not to alarm him. "You're not in trouble, Jake. But your family needs to know who I am and what you and I are up to with the neighbors in the garden."

"My cousin Robin's already told my mom all about it. She's cool with it."

"But I'm not cool with how things stand, Jake. Let's go."

Jake was as skittish as a scared rabbit, his reluctance palpable to Mr. Adams as they walked for several blocks to Jake's home. Jake signaled directions wordlessly at the intersections with mere a nod of his head right or left. When they reached a squat, vinyl-sided apartment building, Jake mounted the steps and drew a key from his pocket, then held the door open for Mr. Adams. Stale smells of tobacco, weed, cat piss, and cooking met them in the dreary hallway. Mr. Adams followed Jake silently up three flights to the door of his flat. Jake opened the door without a key.

Inside, Mr. Adams was relieved to see that the furnishings, though spare, were tidy and clean. He glanced into an empty kitchen as Jake gestured for him to sit on a sofa in the flat's small living room. Next to him on the sofa was a neatly folded sheet and blanket. He suspected he was sitting in Jake's bedroom.

"My mom's probably asleep, sorry," mumbled Jake, clearly embarrassed. "She doesn't get up much. It's been like that since my dad died. She's sad is all."

Mr. Adams wished he'd grasped what he should have before putting Jake through the shame of showing him firsthand. No one knew better than he about the thrall that grief can have on the one left behind by death. Would he have risen out of bed to take care of a daughter if she survived with him? He couldn't say, and wouldn't judge Jake's mother for not being able to be there for her son. How long had Jake been taking care of her? Mr. Adams held his feelings in check. The last thing Jake needed was the burden of Mr. Adams's own grief—or worse, the humiliation if Jake misinterpreted his sadness for pity.

"It's fine, Jake. Get me a pen and paper and I'll write her a note so she knows how to reach me. Also, I want her to know you're joining us for the church pageant and Lotte's party tonight, if you're up for it." Mr. Adams took Jake's shrug as a resounding yes.

NINA

Nina was still in her bathrobe and cozy puffball slippers after a leisurely brunch alone with the newspaper and a latte made with her new Bambino espresso maker—Marty's extravagant Christmas present for her. She decided to take advantage of Raul's absence to wrap presents before he and Marty returned from their annual all-day last minute Christmas Eve shopping ritual. Hastily, she placed her brunch dishes into the sink and scooped her work piles off the dining room table. From her bedroom closet upstairs, she brought the bags of gifts she'd been storing out of sight for weeks, along with cheery rolls of red, green, and silver tissue paper and matching tinsel-y ribbons.

Presents from Raul's "Santa list" took up most of the table space. Marty and she split the list each year after reviewing it together for suitability and their budgets. Marty, always the nice guy, selected the pricey items from the list to buy, and ever since the Santa myth was busted, they left the wrapping to Nina so Raul wouldn't know who gave what. Nina was especially pleased with the Baby-G watch she'd found for Raul. The watch's clear plastic face had knobs to select the date, day of the week, and who-knew-what. She'd had to go all over town to find the Poo-chi Dog he wanted—a strangely captivating, little, robot-y, plastic thing with movable parts that was all the rage among teens that year. But this was nothing compared to the heroic effort she made scouring more than a dozen shoe shops before finding a pair of Heelys, sneakers with rollers built into the heel so they doubled as skates. She hadn't been so lucky in her search for an oversized Paul Frank T-shirt with the big-mouthed monkey face. Only at the last moment had a former client saved her butt, cautioning Nina that she didn't want to know the T-shirt's provenance. Nina was completely okay with this.

She knew Raul would be totally psyched with Marty's indulgences too—the Apple iPod mini 30GB, a Canon digital camera, a massive stack of blank CDs, and a memory card for the camera. They'd nixed getting the Razor scooter, hoping to pick one up for Raul's next birthday when the price would come down. Nina put her foot down about getting Raul the Nintendo DS to play New Super Mario Bros., but Raul went around her objection and bought the set for himself. Amy had taken her side, Nina was glad to learn. But it seemed Amy didn't hold any more sway than she did on the matter.

Nina wrapped her gifts for Amy next. Knowing that Marty's girlfriend had a sweet tooth, she'd bought an expensive box of Recchiuti's chocolates for her. She found a gorgeous blue-and-turquoise, Etro-printed, silk scarf with an exotic garden theme for Amy. A classy gesture—intended as a peace offering of sorts for the admittedly ungracious way Nina initially treated the poor woman. Though they hadn't become what anyone would call close, Nina acknowledged that Amy was a good sport about their unusual family arrangement. More to the point, it seemed Amy was there to stay—at least for the time being—and, as Raul pointed out months earlier, it behooved Nina to come around to accepting this fact.

On fire, she'd banged out the remaining presents with only four more to wrap when the phone rang. She picked up the receiver, not at all happy about interrupting her momentum—and never expecting it would be Horace Moon.

"Nina? Ace here. Hey, how 'bout I come over?"

Like that he asks? Nina fumed silently, annoyed and

speechless. *Like nothing's happened? Like his "How 'bout I come over?" wouldn't be one presumptuous big deal?* After the wild ride at the city's Tax Sale earlier in the month, Nina had made it crystal clear in no uncertain words that things between them were over, done, *finito*. Ace hadn't been in touch and so she assumed he felt the same. And now this call, out of the blue…

She sighed. It made no sense, but she was more than a little intrigued to hear his voice, not that she would admit this to him. She'd missed their fun tug-of-war assignations—and frankly, also, the sex. Maybe her horoscope that morning in the *Chronicle* was right: "Your cosmic landscape is illuminating the opportunity to clear the air of frustration. You'd do well to open to Neptune's exotic house of adventure, have faith, and trust in the process. Your challenge today, Archer? Take care to communicate."

"Okay," she replied curtly into the phone. To herself and the planets, she added, *Here goes trusting in the process, Neptune.*

"Great," Ace answered enthusiastically. "Your address? I can be there in a few minutes."

"What do you mean? Now?"

"Well, I figured you live near the garden, so I'm parked here now on Chula Lane." After she gave him her address, he added, "See you in a jiffy."

Nina hung up, thinking, *Jiffy? I'm about to let a man into my house who uses words like jiffy?* She tugged her bathrobe tighter and ran her hands through her hair as a substitute for a brush. Her mind spun back to the Tax Sale, the last time she'd seen Ace. She'd been disappointed when something came up at work so that Marty wasn't able to be there with them, but he'd coached her, Lotte, Mrs. Hatfield, and Mr. Adams on what to expect and how to bid and sent them off on their own, confident they'd do fine.

As Marty warned, the scene inside the Board of Supervisors' largest meeting room was tense. Each of the gardeners clutched an auction paddle with a number, which they had received after registering outside the meeting room in the historic rotunda, under its gold-painted dome. Marty had advised them not to sit together but to spread out in the room so their paddles would have a better chance of being chosen by the auctioneer. He explained that things would move along scary-fast, but fortunately there were plenty of other properties before their lot #78 was called. By then, they'd get the hang of how to jump into the fray.

Not meaning to, Nina caught Supervisor Riley's attention where he sat on the dais at the front of the room, among his colleagues, behind the railing that separated them from the hoi polloi. He winked at her and Nina shrank lower in the hard, pew-like bench. Marty had assured her that it was fine for her to bid at the auction, as any other citizen could. Being such a public figure, she felt uncomfortable in this setting with so many politicos present. However, this discomfort paled when the man she was secretly sleeping with, Ace, entered the room.

At a glance, she could tell by his posture that Ace was in his element. Unlike how she felt, he seemed completely at ease in this place. He was dressed in a simply tailored, black, cashmere sportscoat, a pressed, white oxford shirt, and no tie. Tall, gorgeous, and casually aristocratic, down to his perfectly fitting, pressed Levis. Trying to be as inconspicuous as possible, Nina watched him from behind her program as he whispered to four sketchy men. They fanned out through the room with their paddles when Ace signaled with a quick lift of his chin, a characteristic gesture of command she knew well. Sizing up Ace's minions by their down-at-the-heels clothing and stooped posture, Nina figured they were one-off hires, probably paid in cash—deadbeats looking to make a quick buck. It seemed that, in his line of work, he—like her—wasn't put off by what others might consider low-life company.

It felt like no time passed when suddenly Nina heard the auctioneer announce that bidding on Lot #78 was to commence, for the vacant lot at the corner of Chula Lane and Abby Street. *Power up,* she coached herself and pulled new Ray Bans from her purse. Changing her mind, she put back the dark glasses—too ostentatious. Better to blend in as best she could, sit back, and chill. She and her friends were as ready as they'd ever be, come what may.

As she expected, the opening bid was $150,000 to cover back taxes, interest, and costs. None of the gardeners' paddles were chosen for the bid, but they were in the running. They had money, thanks to the Foundation's grant. Nina nodded quickly across the room to Lotte, who smiled back with her usual alert and steady demeanor. Nina readied herself to raise her paddle again the moment the auctioneer finished rattling through his rhythmic filler words.

"One-fifty thousand, one-fifty thousand, do I hear two hundred? Two hundred thousand?"

Nina's paddle rose with at least thirty other paddles around the room. The auctioneer quickly carried his chant onto $250,000, and then $300,000. The auctioneer raised the next bid up to $400,000, meaning that next he'd likely next call $500,000, the gardeners' maximum.

Mrs. Hatfield's number was chosen. "My God, we got it!" Nina shouted out loud, immediately embarrassed by her outburst. She hazarded a glimpse at Supervisor Riley who gave her a thumbs-up, which he hastily changed to a resigned shoulder shrug as the bid climbed yet higher.

"She said five-fifty thousand," rattled the auctioneer. "Will you gimme six hundred thousand? Six hundred, even dollar. Would-a-bid six hundred thousand?" Nina frowned. They'd lost the garden by $100,000, in one nerve-wracking instant. She shoved her paddle into her purse. There was no more money to make another bid. It was all over.

Nina made room as Lotte wedged in next to her on the bench. She followed Lotte's head gesture, motioning for her to look in the back corner of the room where a tall, dignified, white-haired woman stood with a raised paddle.

Lotte whispered into Nina's ear, "Something's happening. I can't figure it out. That's Antoinette Moon, and she just won the round."

The room was silent but for the rapid-fire sound of the auctioneer's chant, "I have six hundred thousand, will you give me eight hundred thousand?" The crowd gasped at the size of the auctioneer's jump in price. "Eight hundred thousand! Going once, going twice…" Nina scanned the audience to see who'd won the bid. The auctioneer quickly amended with a flourish, "No, no, no—not over yet, are we? Now who will…will you give me nine hundred thousand? Do I hear nine hundred…?"

Ace's paddle shot up, joined by his mother's and an Asian man Nina didn't recognize. Only these three remained in the competition. The Asian man dropped his paddle after the auctioneer's nod toward Ace's, but Antoinette raised her paddle again and the auctioneer's next bid rose to $1,000,000. Mother and son were bidding against one another. Their fight went on for three more breathtaking rounds, with Lotte's grip on Nina's hand tighter and tighter. Then, suddenly, it was finished.

"Going once, going twice...sold!"

Antoinette carried the sale at $1,300,000. Ace tossed his paddle to the floor. Pale, he rushed out of the room.

Minutes later, in the hallway, the stunned gardeners gathered around Antoinette. She rebuffed an earnest young reporter with a sharp glance. When he backed off, she introduced the gardeners to the man dressed in a tidy black suit who stood at her side, "This is Mr. Rissen, my associate. He'll help you from now on with a Quit Claim Deed for the lot and anything else you need. The grant is yours. Keep it. The garden is safe.

"It has given me no pleasure to humiliate my son in public. But the onus is mine. Who but I raised such a greedy boy?" Nina felt intelligent, sad eyes gazing at her pointedly as Antoinette said, "I've not given up on him yet. I dearly hope you won't, either."

THE SWEET FOLLY OF HOPE

-

Nina's doorbell chimed. As if cued up by planetary conjunctions, Ace was beckoning to her through the glass window in her front door. She tightened her arms across her body to suppress the unbidden urge to smother Ace with kisses, and instead met him with a curt welcome.

"Uh-huh, what do you want?"

Blazing his irresistible, wicked grin, he seemed oblivious to her unfriendly greeting. "I was hoping you'd take the side of, you know...'innocent until proven guilty?'"

"Innocent? You?" She choked back laughter. But before she could say more about the absurdity of this point, he beat her to it.

"You're correct. After the age of six, in humans, innocence is relative. In my case, maybe wind that chronology back to three. But in any case, Counselor, you of all people—defender of much badder people than me—you must find it in your heart to give a guy at least the chance of a fair hearing. Doesn't my sincerity carry some weight?"

Nina rolled her eyes and took a step back. She placed her hands on her hips, trying to pose tough. If he stood any closer to her, she'd drag him upstairs to bed. His fresh smell and the slight dampness of his hair tucked behind his ear brought back intimate images of him stepping out of the shower, naked.

"I can see you're busy," he observed, his eyes taking in her home's open floor plan and the wrapping on the table behind her. "I won't take much time, I promise."

Nina watched with amusement as Ace drew a folded yellow page from his sportsjacket pocket. "A list?" she guffawed and gestured for him to continue. "You do know my soft spots, don't you?"

"I memorized it so I wouldn't need to read it. Here, you take it for later, for reference." When Nina refused his offer, he lay the list on a nearby chair. Then, puffed up like a schoolboy orator, he began. "Number One: The two most important women in my life, my mother and you, aren't speaking to me. Two: It's Christmas, and Jesus was born so that we'd be nicer to one another."

Nina couldn't help interrupting, "And you're hoping to ride his coattails…?"

"Yes, in a word. Yes." Ace grinned. "Please don't interrupt me, or I'll forget the order of my logic. Number three: I didn't bring a present because I knew you'd find it presumptuous. But…number four, I do have a proposition."

Nina glared at him as he nimbly amended, "Not that kind of proposition although rest assured, it's never far from my mind. No, this proposition isn't mine alone. Mother suggested I consider the idea. I have, and I like it...a lot, and thought you might too."

With a flourish, Ace opened one end of the cardboard tube he was carrying. He carefully tapped out what Nina recognized was an architectural sketch. Without asking for her permission, he strode to her table, shoved aside her wrappings, and unrolled the drawing, weighing the corners down with her scissors, coffee cup and two wrapped presents. Despite her irritation with his steamrolling, she was curious. The schema showed a rendering of what was clearly their garden, but showing a one-story building tucked along most of the north side by the alley.

Pointing to the building, Ace said, "These are three, affordable, wheelchair-accessible, studio units, on the north side so the garden's not shaded. You won't believe me, and I get why, but the building I had in mind originally for the lot was to be 100 percent for affordable housing. This plan pares it back to three units instead of thirty, but so what? Safe shelter for thirty families...or a community garden and home for three people?" Ace spread his arms wide and swayed back and forth. "You're the legal expert on weighing the balance point in such immeasurable dilemmas, so I won't say more."

Despite herself, Nina found herself intrigued with the building's attractive image, and knowing how scarce accessible housing was in the city, Nina gave him a genuine smile. The idea had merit.

He forged ahead. "I ask only that I have a public role in the project. I have some pride, as you know. Being publicly burned by my mother was rough. Family therapy would have gouged a hell of a lot less from my inheritance. But, bygones and all that... Taking credit for a public deed like this will help bind the wounds.

"Oh—and did I also say that I'd pay for it? Me, plus tax credits and federal HUD funds, of course. Plus, I get to work with the gardeners on design. They own the land now. Maybe they'll be interested in the idea of a community land trust for the units, or something like that, to handle rents. Most important is...I get to be with you, again."

Nina was surprised to see tears welling from the corners of his eyes. He wiped them impatiently with his sleeve. Contrary to her resolve, her heart softened. She almost reached out to touch his arm, but thought better of it. She knew where that would lead. Better to keep her distance.

Before she could respond, he jumped in with, "Even if you don't think it'll fly with everyone—and I'm betting it will—please, please, please let me know when we can kiss again."

Nina felt his blue, blue eyes boring into hers, and

she melted a bit closer to the puddle of mush she knew she would turn into if she didn't get a grip on things. She sat down hard and tried to look like she wasn't affected in the slightest by his question.

"I miss your kisses," he continued, seemingly undaunted by her severe affect. "I miss doing whatever we call talking—arguing, playing our word fights. I miss our walks, fondling your amazing body on the plaid blanket behind the Verdi statue like teenagers, signing in as Mr. and Mrs. Brown for life-altering trysts in Capitola's finest Motel-6.

"I miss you. Nina, I like you…a lot. 'Just friends' will never be sufficient, but if that's all I get this Christmas, it's bounty enough…for now."

He'd bulldozed his way right into her heart once more, and done again what few others had achieved—sent her mind spinning and her mouth speechless.

"Gone quiet, I see," observed Ace. "That's fine. I've said my bit. Best I go, right?" He answered himself. "Right. Call me. Please."

His car door closed before her wits returned. She rolled the sketch into its sleeve and set it next to the stack of case files piled beside the couch. Momentarily, she mulled over the double whammy ahead of her—when the site drawings were eventually shared, she'd also have to reveal her secret relationship with Ace to Raul, Marty, Lotte, and everyone else. *Ah well…* she sighed. Time enough after the holidays to see how everything unfolds.

Then, laughing at the absurdity of it all, she called into the empty house, "'Neptune's exotic house of adventure,' you betcha…Game is most definitely on!"

LIZ

iz arrived at the church early, with Allegra, Lotte, Vince, and Anna in tow. Stepping through the church doors, Liz let go of Allegra's hand so she could dash off with other children to the church basement in preparation for the pageant. Twelve months earlier, Liz could never have imagined Allegra so filled with confident energy and laughter, nor herself sitting on a church pew, let alone next to a half-sister, or "new sister," as she and Anna preferred to call their relationship. "Half" made something sound incomplete, they agreed, while in truth it felt quite the opposite. Since their first disastrous introduction over the phone, Liz was blown away by how much more whole she was with Anna in her life, as if she completed a part of Liz that long felt empty and unfinished.

Liz felt Anna's hand squeeze hers as if to confirm her thoughts. She settled in closer to her on the pew and sighed.

"What is it?" whispered Anna.

Liz shrugged and said evasively. "I don't know. I don't really want to talk about it. Let's be happy, yes? Or as best we can." The last thing she wanted was to bring down the Christmas cheer by sharing what was eating her. She clutched her purse in her lap and wished its contents would magically vanish.

Liz was grateful for Anna' easy smile. "Fine by me. I am happy. I was just thinking about us, and how remarkable it is we made it through that first dinner at Lotte's. And how glad I am we did."

"Oh God!" exclaimed Liz. "Allegra was like a dog with a bone. She wouldn't let up until I agreed to that dinner. Lotte was no help, either. The two of them ganged up on me, literally dragging my ass to the table. Did you know we planned it in Lotte's loft so I could make a quick exit upstairs if the whole thing backfired?"

Liz shook her head in wonder, recollecting her initial reluctance. She told Anna how, as the evening approached, Allegra's persistent questioning and giddiness only increased Liz's apprehension. Lotte insisted on Allegra's favorites for the menu: mac and cheese with apple juice and pistachio ice cream cones for dessert. While Liz sulked, the two of them spent hours creating a colorful mural for the front door. Bright, crayoned letters spelled out "Welcome Aunt Anna" above a replica of the garden with pink and yellow flowers and purple vegetables.

"Allegra nearly burst open with impatience to show her new aunt the rivers of ants she drew across the bottom of the banner in your honor."

"Neither of us spoke to one another through the entire meal," said Anna, laughing. "I was afraid you'd throw your plate at me if I even so much as asked you to pass the salt and pepper."

"Thank God for Allegra," sighed Liz. "Remember how she filled in our silences with her endless chatter about one thing or another? I felt so humiliated letting her, once again, smooth over my inadequacies."

"We've her and Lotte to thank for beginning to sing after dinner. Everything shifted then, didn't it?" said Anna. "You and I spontaneously joined in on the harmony."

"That was really amazing, how our voices blended," recalled Liz. "We pulled off some pretty fancy harmonies too, didn't we?"

By Allegra's bedtime, Lotte was hoarse and everyone's mood was high. They'd run through "Baa Baa Black Sheep," "Row, Row, Row Your Boat," and many others, including a couple of rounds that Anna taught them from her childhood. After the finale of "Dona Nobis Pacem," Anna joined Liz and Allegra upstairs where, together, they tucked a tired, very happy Allegra into bed.

The sisters' reminiscences broke off when Liz heard agitated voices and scuffling behind their pew. She turned to look. Two rows back, in the aisle, Nina was squared-off in front of her teenage son Raul, one hand holding him by the elbow of his jacket sleeve. Mr. Adams stood between Raul and another boy who Liz recognized as Jake, Allegra's surly friend from the garden. Mr. Adams's hands were firmly on the two teens' shoulders, keeping them separate.

She heard Nina's exasperated tone as conversation ceased throughout the church and all eyes turned toward the interruption. "Yes, you will apologize this very moment young man."

"All I said was 'What are you doing here?'" Liz caught the sound of Raul's whining defense as he shook his arm from Nina's tight grasp and grumbled, "Let go, Mom. You're making a scene. It's no big deal, right Jake?"

Liz squelched a sympathetic giggle as she watched her tiny friend Nina stamp a spiked heel on the floor to keep her son's attention. Raul, six inches taller after the year's growth spurt, loomed above his mother, but there was no doubt who was in charge of the moment.

"Your tone was not welcoming, Raul," scolded Nina. "We're in church and it's Christmas Eve, remember? Now do the right thing and apologize to Jake so we can all sit down."

"It's cool, Mrs. Reynos. Merry Christmas," Liz heard Jake interject.

She hadn't heard this tone of voice from Jake before, and its sweetness came as a surprise. He didn't sound the least bit like his usual snarky self. But, Liz observed, while his voice may have softened, his appearance hadn't. He was dressed in his unchanging uniform of baggy black clothing. She noticed a creepy spider tattoo on his neck, crawling from the top of his T-shirt toward stringy hair that begged for some water and shampoo.

"Hey...man, right on. Merry Christmas, Mom," added Raul.

"Jake, you're coming to sit with us, okay?" Nina's invitation sounded to Liz more like a command than an option.

Jake's puzzled look moved from Nina to Raul to Mr. Adams. Raul appeared plainly reluctant still, but with a nudge in his side from Nina, he signaled Mr. Adams with one thumb up and Nina marched both boys up the aisle. She stopped in front of the empty pew across the aisle from Liz and pointed the way in for each boy to sit. Liz caught Nina's eye and reached out her hand.

"Where's Allegra?" whispered Nina, leaning in and offering both cheeks for Liz to kiss. "I've corralled both her boyfriends onto the same pew."

"She's backstage. One of the angels. My daughter…an angel?"

"Honey, all I can say is to relish the angel years. Believe me, all too soon they're long gone and forgotten memories. Hey, listen—Lotte knows, but I wanted you to know, too. Sorry to miss the party tonight. We've got to scoot home after this for dinner at Marty's. Family tradition and all…"

Liz felt Anna nudge her shoulder and she turned to see Mr. Adams entering on the other end of their pew. He squeezed in front of Vince's knees which looked awfully close to Lotte's and then waited for Vince to take his nose out of a hymnal and move aside so he could sit next to Lotte.

Much to Liz's amusement, Nina rolled her eyes and remarked about this mini-drama unfolding before them, "Men? And…boys. You gotta love 'em, the poor dears." Vigorous nods from Lotte, Anna, and Liz confirmed that Nina's point was well taken.

When Nina took her seat across the aisle, Anna said, "She seems fun. One tough cookie, you can tell."

"She is, on both counts," agreed Liz. "Nina's with the public defender's office and she's a good friend. You're really going to love her."

Liz told Anna about Allegra's big crush on Raul and how she'd bent to Allegra's pleading to attend Holy Innocents, where the garden planning committee met and where Raul and Nina were regulars. Molly Rengate, the church's eccentric minister, had become another friend who Liz wanted Anna to meet. It was Molly who invited her to join Nina and other churchwomen in their Wednesday noon book group. "We sit on lumpy sofas in the basement and talk about all kinds of things. Sometimes, even the *Bible*. When we get tired of that, we read novels and talk about how come our lives have or haven't turned out like fiction. We call ourselves the So-Fah-So-Goods...the sofas, get it?" Liz made a point of stretching out the group's name so Anna wouldn't miss the corny pun. "'We're all works in progress,' says Molly."

"Got that right."

Liz felt a sisterly punch on her shoulder, and she playfully pecked Anna's cheek. "Church is a first for me, you know. But I like it, in my skittish kind of way." She confessed to Anna, "My faith, if you can call it that, is wobbly at best. But I like how we laugh a lot here on Sunday mornings. Something always busts me up. I also end up crying—not that anyone seems to mind, or even notice. They welcome all comers, I guess. I really love the singing, too. Everybody belts out the hymns loud and off-key. You'll see. I get a kick seeing Allegra stand on the pew to sing hymns without knowing the tune or language."

Liz explained that because Molly learned Spanish in Honduras as a Peace Corps volunteer—and kept it up through her community work—church services at Holy Innocents were casually bilingual, with an equal mix of Spanish and English speakers. Parts of the service were translated into both languages, and others not. Lacking Spanish, Liz had no idea what she was missing or what she was reciting or singing much of the time. Like in her AA meetings, Liz found herself warming to people's affection, bit by bit… "a work in progress."

"Maybe someday I could come to your SoFa group?" asked Anna. "It sounds like I'd fit right in, but I know I have to *couch* my request."

"Ouch." Liz mock-grimaced. "I've told them all about you, of course. The whole saga…but hey, don't worry." Reading Anna's alarmed expression, Liz explained, "You come out sounding like the good daughter, not like me at all. Anyway, when you visit the SoFas you'll see how messed up all our lives are."

Liz recounted the day when she whined about not having a normal family and the SoFas had piped up with stories of their own families' disarray. One friend's mother-in-law had recently moved in, along with nine cats and an orchid collection. Another told a hilarious story about her husband's smell after three months of not bathing, a biology experiment for his masters degree. Molly regaled them with a description of the confused police officer who begged her to remove her daughter from the station steps where she was picketing unfair treatment of street jugglers.

Liz stopped short. A cocktail of suppressed rage, guilt and fear surged through her. She closed her eyes, trying to pull herself together.

"What's wrong?"asked Anna.

"Nothing," snapped Liz. But the letter in her purse was anything but nothing. It was from Jonathan, Allegra's father. The same Jonathan who'd been dead to her for over six years. The Jonathan she'd told Allegra was dead. Over Lotte's objections and many lectures about the dangers of deception, Liz finally persuaded Lotte to promise to back her up. From what she could tell, Allegra took her father's death in stride, never once asking her about him. This was fine with Liz. She had hoped to keep it that way.

After a hasty glance at the letter's content that morning, Liz had stuffed it into her purse. The many details required for Allegra's costume and script; invitations for Lotte's party and arranging for the piano player; practicing the song she and Anna were going to sing at the party; doing the laundry; last minute shopping; and squeezing in an AA meeting had proved sufficient distraction for Liz to slip into an oblivion of denial.

She fumbled in her purse for the letter to show Anna, and then thought better of it. Along with an apology, Jonathan sent a cashier's check for $120,000, twenty thousand dollars for each of Allegra's years. Because of his work in international philanthropy he'd been tapped to help get a new foundation off the ground in Seattle. He wanted to meet Allegra and be in her life. The money, he said, wasn't contingent on this. He understood if Liz didn't allow it. He'd keep sending money each year, more if needed. He wished he'd done it earlier.

Anna leaned in and asked, "What's going on? You look weird. Everything Okay?"

"Jonathan…" Liz whispered the name through gritted teeth. She gestured with a finger to her lips for Anna to keep quiet. Either she continued living the lie of Jonathan's death or opened a way for something else to happen. Was her sobriety up for this?

On autopilot, she ticked through her gratitude list: she was sober, surrounded by people who loved her, bolstered by her special relationship with her Sponsor, Nick…

Inhaling deeply, the decision hit her. She could do this. She could and would walk through the wall of pretense she'd trapped Allegra and Lotte in, somehow redeem herself with them for her past lies and, most importantly, provide a chance for Allegra to know her father. She gripped Anna's hand firmly with hers and whispered, "Not now, not here, but soon, I promise. I'm gonna need your help with something. I can't do it alone, but this stays between us until I say."

"Got it."

A lively organ riff announced the pageant's start and spared Liz from going any further. She felt the press of Anna's hand in hers as they stood for the procession. She could trust Anna not to pry and knew her secret was safe for a while longer. Recognizing the tune of "O Come All Ye Faithful" Liz smiled, brushing away Anna's offer of a hymnal. The previous weeks' daily practice with Allegra brought the hymn's words in English and Spanish easily to mind.

Liz turned to the back of the church where the rustle of small costumed shepherds, the jingle of three leashed dogs dressed as lambs, and a wandering chicken could be heard as they made haphazard progress down the aisle. Parents' coos turned to gasps as one overly exuberant dog jumped to hump another and a shepherd tripped on the dog's leash as its owner tried to restrain it. But not to worry. The fallen shepherd caught himself and stood up without missing a beat, the dogs wagged their tails, and a crowd of angels pressed the shepherds forward up the aisle.

Liz sighted Allegra and waved. Allegra waved back so wildly that one of the older angels needed to re-adjust a fallen wing

ALLEGRA

How come those two are together? wondered Allegra, frowning as she made her way slowly up the aisle toward Jake and Raul. She tried her best not to look at them or at her Mom, Anna, and Lotte, who were blowing kisses, trying to get her attention on the other side of the aisle. *I'm not going to wave at them again,* she thought, worried that her floppy wings would fall apart if she moved her arm up to throw a kiss back.

Allegra hoped Jake wouldn't tell Raul about the Snail Palace. It was their secret, even though Mr. Adams and Lotte found out. She hadn't told her mother anything about it, and promised herself that she wouldn't because it was none of Liz's business. Continuing up the aisle, she pressed her blunt fingernails into the tight ball of her left fist, silently repeated the words she'd memorized and tried not to trip on the trailing edge of a king's green velvet train.

How'd the three kings get ahead of her? They were 'sposed to be following *behind* the angels. There were only two kings and they were boys, not men kings. All dressed up with their crowns, fake beards, and powdered hair, Allegra thought they did kind of look like kings, but they didn't act like kings. Allegra stole a quick look behind her to make sure the Virgin Mary and Joseph were coming up the aisle, still. Yup, there they were. The Virgin Mary was carrying a real baby. But this, like the kings, was messed up, too. The baby was a girl baby. Earlier, she told the Virgin Mary it should be a boy baby. The Virgin Mary told Allegra it didn't matter, 'cause it was pretend. But it did matter to Allegra. Jesus was a boy.

She returned to worrying about how come Jake and Raul were suddenly friends. She hoped they'd still be her friend, too, and wished she could be a boy, sometimes. Like worms are sometimes girls, and sometimes boys. All the shepherds and both kings were boys. Girls only got to be angels or the Virgin Mary. It wasn't fair.

Seconds before Allegra and the other angels reached the three steps up to the altar—where a child's car seat sat on a bed of hay—she heard Molly at the back of the church calling out, "Rejoice! *¡Regocijarse!*"

Allegra found her place on the top step next to a boy who said his name was Roger, and that he was the brother of one of the big angels. Dressed in a bathrobe like the other shepherds, Roger was holding a white dog with beady black eyes and a brown spot on its head. Allegra looked up from the dog in time to see two of the big angels step forward in front.

One angel said, "Unto us is born a Savior!"

The other angel repeated in Spanish, *"¡El Salvador, se nace!"*

This was everyone's signal to sit, Allegra remembered and poked Roger next to her to sit. He did, but his strange-eyed dog wouldn't sit, and it made Allegra nervous. So, she inched down a step closer to the Virgin Mary to get away from it. She saw the Virgin Mary pull a pacifier from her blue robe and put it near the baby girl Jesus in the car seat manger. When the choir began to sing, Roger's dog barked and everyone laughed, except Allegra, who didn't think it was funny. *Stupid old dog,* she thought, glad she wasn't beside it anymore.

Once the choir sat, the tallest angel raised her hand and Allegra tightened her fists again, knowing her time was coming. Like they practiced, she followed behind her new friend, Mimi—who everyone called Goldilocks because of the yellow hair Allegra wished she had—and joined with the other angels to make a half-circle behind Mary and Joseph. Allegra took two stiff steps forward, holding Mimi's hand.

She stopped breathing, frozen. She couldn't remember what she was 'sposed to say. She opened her mouth, but nothing came out. When Mimi tugged on her hand, Allegra bit her lip. All of a sudden, double-quick from way down inside her and out through her mouth came the lost words, strong and exactly like they were supposed to: *"¡Mira! ¡El ee-ho de Dee-os!"*

When Mimi had her turn saying the same thing in English, Allegra breathed out loudly, relieved they got to sit down again. She would later draw a blank on anything else after that about the pageant, until everyone sang "We Three Kings," one of her favorite carols, and she heard Molly talking about presents.

"Whether it's Christmas, Kwanzaa, or Hanukkah, this season's about presents, *si?"* Molly asked. *"Regalos! Santa Claus va dar* presents, like the kings brought *regalos* for Baby Jesus tonight. So, what's Baby Jesus' present for us?"

Allegra was stumped by the question until she heard Roger the shepherd softly say, "Love."

Molly clapped and said, "Yes! *El regalo de Jesús es su amor.* Jesus's love is here for us every minute of every day, *siempre, cualquiera pasa,* and it is magic. Why? Because it opens our hearts to all the other *regalos* of the world...all of this!" Molly spread her arms out wide and circled slowly. "The pageant, the Christmas story, the candle lights, our families. Everything. Outer space is a gift. Stars, the moon, *el sol*...ah, the marvelous gift of the sun!"

Electrified, Allegra watched Molly laugh and clasp her arms around herself in a tight hug. Then Molly got serious. Her face scrunched up in a frown, worrying Allegra about what might be coming next. And it didn't get better when Molly began to speak.

"Now wait a minute—some things the world gives us, we'd just as soon not get. Maybe your teacher's too hard on you? Thanks, but no thanks for *that* present. Or your best friend goes to live with her dad far away? Or you have to move to a new school where you don't know anyone? Or someone in your family gets very sick? Thanks, but no thanks!" Allegra listened as Molly's voice got quiet and her worried look disappeared. "Thing is, even if everything is horrid, no matter what else is happening in your life, the love of Jesus is right here too. I'm not saying it's always easy to find, but He's here, *siempre*."

Allegra couldn't think of anything to say when Molly called the children to stand up and tell about a time when they felt Jesus' love at the same time the world was giving them a very tough gift. Behind her the shepherd, who was next to Roger—the one with the dog, and who was one of the big angel's brothers—took the microphone Molly handed him. He told how his hamster died but he got a dog instead. Then, to Allegra's disgust, Roger's dog licked the boy's face when he bent down to pat him. Everyone laughed, but Allegra didn't see what was funny. Nor did she understand why everyone also laughed when, next, a king told about how hard it was when his mom and dad got divorced, but then it turned out okay because his dad took him to *X-Men*, a movie his mom said he couldn't see.

"Who else would like to share?" asked Molly. Mimi raised her hand, right next to Allegra who suddenly felt like everyone was watching her.

Mimi pulled on one of her pretty, golden-yellow curls and whispered into the microphone, "Ron, next door, got shot dead."

Allegra shivered when she heard this and didn't know if she should hold Mimi's hand to make her feel better. But she didn't move. No one moved. The church was very quiet, and Molly said like she was going to cry.

"Mimi, I am so very sorry," Molly said. "It must be very hard to find any gift at all from this terrible tragedy." Mimi nodded her head slowly. Allegra held her breath, waiting to hear what Molly would say next. "Thank you, Mimi. It's a gift to all of us that you brought Ron's memory to us tonight, a gift that will remain with me forever." Molly closed her eyes, put her hands together at her heart like an angel does, and bowed to Mimi.

Then Allegra's words wanted to speak too. She stepped forward. Molly leaned forward and held the microphone near Allegra's face. She was about to start when she saw her mom blow her a kiss from her seat, and decided not to tell about New York. "I don't want to tell about the first thing, the bad part."

"Fair enough," said Molly, "Can you say if you felt a gift of love?"

That was easy. "We got to come live with Lotte and make a garden with worms and Mr. Adams, and now my mom's happy."

Allegra wondered how come Molly was crying and smiling at the same time. She saw that Liz and Lotte were crying and smiling too. A second kiss blown from Liz landed on her lips like it was real. Mimi was crying hard, so Allegra reached over and held her hand. She wasn't sure, but it looked like the Virgin Mary's cheeks were wet with tears as she knelt next to the baby girl Jesus, who'd stayed asleep through the whole pageant.

Seeing the Virgin Mary's and everybody else's tears, Allegra started to cry too, for no good reason except it felt good. She wiped her dripping nose on the sleeve of her angel costume. It seemed sometimes big girls do cry, after all.

LOTTE

The loft was already alive with convivial sounds of chatter and laughter when Lotte arrived with Liz, Allegra, Vince, and Anna after the church pageant. She counted several of Liz's friends gathered around a keyboard, recognizing some as co-workers from the bar where Liz sang. Others were less familiar, and Lotte assumed they must be AA friends. The group was singing an exuberant, slightly revised rendition of the familiar carol, "God Rest Ye Merry Gentle... Beasts."

How delighted Lotte was to observe the obvious affection that Liz's friends had for her as they hugged. She watched the piano player, without missing a note, offer his lips for a kiss from Anna—a kiss which seemed, to Lotte, to linger a bit beyond friendly. *Hmmm? Interesting,* she thought, smiling.

All the coat hooks by the door were taken, evidence of a very full house. She noted that Anna and Vince also needed a place for their wet coats and umbrellas and offered to take them to her bedroom with her own. Witnessing his awkward bow, she recalled how Vince always entered a party this way, by shyly retreating to the edges of a gathering. In the past she'd rescued him, helped put him at ease when company was around. She was relieved that Allegra intervened and insisted that Grandaddy and Aunt Anna visit her bedroom first, where they could leave their things.

Lotte took an instant to gather herself with an inhaled breath, then headed slowly toward Henry's less complicated company. He was helping himself to the bounty of potluck snacks that had magically appeared on the center table. She recognized the corner bakery's fancy strawberry cheesecake and what had to be Mrs. Hatfield's piles of homemade cookies and brownies. Someone had added an array of cheese and dip plates next to her own vegetable platter, piled high with carrots, parsnips, cukes, and radishes from the farmer's market. She had sliced and arranged them earlier, glad for the simple activity to ground her roiling emotions after their return from their frenetic search for the missing Allegra.

Dipping a carrot into hummus, she scanned her thoughts for any residue of discomfort that might be skulking inside her from the afternoon. Right away, she'd regretted going with John and the children to that fancy restaurant. Throughout the meal, she felt as uncomfortable as Jake looked. She avoided John's eyes and barely offered a word. But for Allegra's bubbling enthusiasm for everything, lunch would have been a disaster with so much left unsaid cluttering the table. She would have preferred to stay home, alone on her meditation cushion where she could process her emotions so they didn't fester and devour her enjoyment of the evening.

Thank goodness she did find time once the party preparations were done, for it was only in the silent exploration of her feelings while in meditation that she realized how her need to distance herself from John at lunch came not from fear of what might have happened to Allegra. The children were fine. Harder to shrug off was her exasperation with him for letting the children slip out of sight in the first place. She softly probed deeper in silence, as she was practiced in doing, and discovered that underneath her anger with John was embarrassment with her own panic and angry outbursts, and under this... disappointment with herself, for trusting John in the first place. Dismissing the tired old excuse of blaming Vince's betrayals for her distrust, deeper yet she dove into her consciousness with each breath, until the familiar bite of rock bottom fear and grief gripped her and held hard, seeming to gouge out her very being. *Breathe,* she counseled herself gently, and whispered the label "Feelings" to regain perspective. In time, a vast, peaceful openness appeared in their place. Later, in church, in the moment when she opened her hand fully to John's as he reached for hers, she recognized that the penetrating magic of mentally letting go had worked...

Henry's nod and wink across the table caught her eye and delivered her from further reflection. She drew near him, wishing to thank him for championing Jake. The afternoon's visit to Jake's Snail Palace had erased previous doubts about the potential that John saw in the boy.

Hmmm... she wondered, studying Henry, *Had he shaved his beard? Was that a new sports jacket?* The changes in Henry were visibly dramatic since his sculpture was vandalized and re-made. He and his artwork were both transformed. The new fence around the garden was so impressive that a slick city planning magazine gave it a full-color spread, which resulted in two hefty commissions for Henry's playful version of fencing. In the wake of fame, he'd become positively charming. *Well—not quite charming,* Lotte corrected herself as Henry reached a finger deep into his open mouth to dislodge a bit of something.

Drawn instead by the more tasteful sight of Mrs. Hatfield across the room with her gorgeous new great-grandbaby bundled on her lap, Lotte stopped only briefly with Henry to thank him and wish him Merry Christmas.

On her way to Mrs. Hatfield, she recognized another good friend among the piano crowd. "Josie, so wonderful to see you," exclaimed Lotte.

"Thanks for getting me out of the house, Lotte. Only your invitation could budge me from under the rock where I've been hiding. It's weird going anywhere without Paulo, you know? But he always loved a party, so I tucked him somewhere inside, and…came."

"I've missed you. We all have." Lotte welcomed Josie's embrace, and knowing it would lift the mood, said, "Hey, check this out." Angling for a compliment on the first pair of high heels she'd worn in more than a decade, she pointed one foot flirtatiously toward Josie. "Liz made me get them."

To Lotte's pleasure, Josie whistled. "Foxy! Silly me, I thought you were glued into garden clogs, girlfriend. Boy, oh boy was I wrong, wrong, wrong!" It was Lotte's turn to whistle as Josie swirled the slinky silk skirt of her low-cut red dress and kicked out a leg. "Check this out, Lotte. You like? 'Specially for the season. It's my come-out-of-hiding party dress."

"Hmmm…?" joked Lotte as she wittingly stared at Josie's exposed décolletage. "I'd say you are in top form, pun intended."

Then, in asking if Josie was ready to sing with Liz and Anna, she realized from Josie's expression that she probably hadn't heard about Anna, the newest addition to their family. Lotte turned to look for Liz and found her by the food table talking with Nate from the garden. She waved her over. "Liz, can you introduce Josie to Anna?"

"I would love to but last I knew, Allegra was insisting Anna look at something in her room." Liz hugged Josie and said, "You'll never believe what I got for Christmas. A brand-new, grown-up sister. And she sings like a red-hot mama."

Josie clapped her hands. "That makes two red-hot mama-sister singers, then."

"Join us?" pleaded Liz. "We've worked up a bluesy-jazzy something of John Prine's, grooving off Bonnie Raitt's cut of 'Make me an Angel.' I know you know it."

"To die for!" gushed Josie. "But I'll leave it to the *au courant* Andrews sisters. My voice is crusty from disuse. I don't dare sing except in the shower."

"Somehow I can't believe that's true, but know you're welcome to chime in," said Liz, handing Josie the plate of chips she'd brought with her. "Let me find Anna before Allegra demands ransom."

Josie set the chips on a nearby end table and said, "Sing? Not a chance. It's enough I'm out and not home alone on the couch, wailing. This is my first foray into anything more social than the post office."

Seeing Josie's eyes well up, Lotte reached for her hand. "Come. You need a dose of baby."

She led Josie to Mrs. Hatfield where she, her grandson Neilson, and his wife Emma greeted them warmly. Mrs. Hatfield ordered Josie, "Here, sweetie, meet my tiny baby boy."

Clucking at the drowsy newborn nestled in Josie's arms, Lotte felt a tug on her hem. One of Millie Peterson's three children—Lotte could never keep straight which was which—demanded earnestly, "I wonned four presents 'cause I found one hundred and thirteen snails. Ray only found eighty-six."

Lotte assured the child that he and his brother would get their rewards by and by, then turned to the sound of the front doorbell. When Mr. Adams and Jake entered, Lotte heard Allegra cry out, "Zorro!" She smiled as Allegra jumped up and dashed to greet the newcomers. Then she chastened herself for the twinge of satisfaction she felt seeing Vince left in the lurch on the floor alone amidst crayons and loose paper. *Was she ever going to be free from wishing this man pain?*

She looked around for John, but seeing Nate grab

his arm she knew he'd be occupied for a while over some garden matter pressing on Nate's mind. *Oh well,* she thought without disappointment. *There'll be time later. Meanwhile,* Lotte wondered, *who is the elegantly tailored, elderly, Asian couple?* The mystery was solved as Winn, Liz's former voice teacher, and Thea, his wife, entered the loft behind them. Putting two and two together, Lotte figured the unknown couple must be Winn's parents. Thea had begged Lotte for an invitation to the party, explaining she was desperate for a distraction from her difficult in-laws who were staying the week.

Assured that Josie and Mrs. Hatfield were captivated by each other's and the baby's charms, Lotte crossed the room to fill a champagne glass. She welcomed Thea and Winn with kisses and offered handshakes for his more reserved parents. Then she gave Thea a quick lift of her eyebrows to let her old friend know she had the situation in hand. She handed the champagne to Thea who, her other arm weighted with coats, headed knowingly to the bedroom.

"Back in a minute," she said, "after I powder my nose."

Lotte ushered Winn and his parents over to Henry, who was still at the food table, now gobbling a handful of popcorn. "Let me introduce you. Hmmm...Henry is a sculptor of some renown. Henry, Mr. and Mrs.

Liu are from Manhattan. Am I correct in recalling you are in the same brownstone where Winn grew up? He speaks so lovingly of that stately historic home, and of you. Henry, the Lius are influential supporters of the arts. Why don't you tell them about your work..."

She didn't wait to see how the three would mix before leading Winn by the arm toward the piano and singers. "Winn, these kids need your baritone."

"Thank you, darling. I owe you one for this," Winn whispered into her ear.

Laughing, Lotte said, "Wait till you hear Liz and Anna sing tonight, Winn. Turning Liz into a singer is the best payback you could ever give me. Without your encouragement so many years ago..." She left the words hanging and flashed him a knowing smile. "Hmmm...now the only thing I ask is please promise to make sure your folks leave with a one-way ticket home so Thea doesn't leave you first."

As they neared the group, Lotte was taken aback by how much Anna and Liz looked alike. Though of course they would...they were sisters, after all. That evening, their resemblance was accentuated by the similar flair of their saucy, short-cut dresses in shades of green, flawlessly setting off their auburn hair. Lotte marveled at the sight of them so at ease with one another.

Initially when Anna arrived in their lives, Lotte

was conscious of wanting to protect Liz. Anna was an accomplished musician. She'd studied classical viola formally, had her PhD, and was on track for a professorship at Cal State Hayward. Would Liz feel less-than? And then what…? Only when she overheard Anna tell Liz that she was envious of her talent and the guts it took to sing in public did Lotte know she could step back, confident that a growing strength of connection between the sisters would see them through the ups and downs of sibling rivalry, and hopefully…whatever else.

Mid-hug with Anna, Lotte hesitated, wondering how to introduce her to Winn. But before she could come up with anything, Anna introduced herself. "Hi, Winn. I'm Lotte's other daughter."

Touched deeply by Anna's unprompted gift, Lotte smiled and kissed her on the cheek. "I love it…my dearest 'other daughter.'" She explained to Anna how Winn was responsible for Liz's singing. "He's a fabulous baritone in his own right. Winn, didn't you sing with the Opera…*Carmen,* wasn't it?"

"Pure hyperbole," he objected, clearing his throat in an exaggerated manner. "I was a mute, walk-on foot soldier once, more than twelve years ago. Believe me, if I'd let out so much as a squeak the stage director would have personally impaled me on my own bayonet."

Confident that Winn was happy to be enfolded

among Anna and Liz's friends, Lotte took her leave. She stepped to the party's sidelines for a moment's quiet amidst the caroling and conversation. Balanced on the back of an armchair, she slipped off one and then the other glittery, high-heeled shoe. Her toes, unaccustomed to being confined within such stylishness, relaxed with instant relief. She pushed the shoes under the chair so no one would trip.

"Sexy heels."

Lotte heard Vince's voice coming from the other side of the chair. Twisting around, she found him on the floor where she last saw him, when Allegra took off to greet Jake. Vince held one of her shoes in his hand. She shivered in repugnance. Was his thumb actually rubbing the heel of the shoe?

"Vince, put that down," she ordered. The shoe fell with a thud on the floor.

"We're a family, Lotte," he said softly, requiring her to bend toward him to hear and annoying her further.

Vince, seemingly oblivious to her vexation, waved his hand vaguely. Lotte supposed he meant for her to take in the scene around them but was unprepared for his next words.

"I'm so grateful to you. Molly said it all tonight in church. You are a gift. Dare I say God's gift?"

Lotte winced internally and tried not to show her confusion.

"Or 'Buddha's gift,' better said, yes? My words don't convey it well, Lotte, but I mean it. Thank you."

She wished she could take him at his word, but trusting Vince never seemed wise. Was he being ironic or sincere? His smile felt more to her like an obsequious smirk than genuine. She bit her tongue, suppressing words that would sully the evening even further than Vince's unwelcome gesture with her shoe.

"They sound good, don't they?" Vince asked, as Liz, Anna, and the piano player started up the piece they'd practiced for the evening.

On this, Lotte could wholeheartedly agree. She would have said as much, but wouldn't have been heard. So instead of trying, she gave way to the music. Wow! The interplay of their three voices alloyed together in jazzy, discordant harmonies and resonated with surprising syncopations. They were electrifying, thrilling. Lotte's heart jumped into her throat when the trio invited their audience to sing with them on a final round of the song's plea to...

> "...Just give me one thing
> That I can hold on to
> To believe in
> This livin'
> Is just a hard way to go"

-

By the time everyone's uproarious applause ended, all of Lotte's ill will toward Vince was erased. She turned to share her pride with him. But before she could, Allegra dive-bombed into his lap.

"I'm gonna vomit," Allegra groaned. "Cookies… ughhhh."

Doubly worried for Allegra and that she might be sick on Vince's cashmere sports jacket, Lotte knelt, intending to take her from him.

Vince shook his head and laughed. "Not on your life, Lotte. I've got this one. One hundred percent. Trust me."

Allegra fell instantly asleep, her color returning quickly, safely held in her Grandaddy's arms.

Tears brimming, Lotte stood and looked away, and…there was John. He was leaning against the wall near the window by her meditation cushion, across the room. His smile felt warm and kind. She caught his eye and smiled back. He shrugged in that good-natured way of his, and she knew instantly where she'd head next.

As she moved closer, John extended both hands to greet her. She readily accepted them in hers.

"You did that well," he commented.

"Hmmm…?" Lotte queried, wondering what

exactly she did well. Had he witnessed her flare-up with Vince over the shoe, Allegra's collapse, or was he alluding to her eager response when he reached to welcome her? Perhaps he was feeling similar sensations through the weave of their fingers. She felt in his hands a comfortable firmness that sent a sweet tangle of emotions flashing through her.

"You help people find their place," he clarified.

"Not sure what you mean?" She was genuinely baffled, but from his kind eyes she knew he meant it as a compliment. She waited for him to explain.

John laughed gently, "I've been watching you. It's impressive, and I bet you don't even know what it is you are doing. Here..." He paused, dropping his hands to pass his glass of soda water and lime to her. "You must be thirsty."

"Thanks, I am." Taking a sip before handing it back, Lotte wondered how John knew this was her favorite drink. She surmised Liz and John must be conspiring behind her back. "But I'm still not clear what you mean."

"Within minutes of arriving in the room," Mr. Adams replied, "I saw you touch everyone in welcome as you helped them feel at home. Look for yourself at the results." She felt his hands brace her shoulders lightly as he turned her to face in the direction of where Josie and Mrs. Hatfield were head-to-head over the baby.

Lotte laughed. "That's nice of you to say. But honestly, I didn't do anything. Those two are in love with one another. They've both got hearts as big as the moon."

"From my experience, it's not simply a matter of bringing people into the same room, no matter how big their hearts. Much depends on the convener's magic. Look what unexpected healing happened just today in Jake's hideout, despite my own ineptitude. Your being with us made all the difference."

Lotte avoided meeting John's eyes, worried that he might be indirectly acknowledging that he wanted to talk about their afternoon's mishap. She no longer had any regrets to unearth. And besides, everything had more than worked out for the better.

She needn't have feared. Mr. Adams was steering their conversation to an observation about his father. "In any case, as I was saying, my father called gifts such as yours, 'knacks.' He himself had a knack for woodcarving. Nothing could stop him from whittling, and he whittled with style, hardly knowing he was doing it half the time. Up, out of his hands came a carved knob on a walking stick, a whistle, a toothpick, or what have you."

"Hmmm..." replied Lotte, enjoying the ease she felt in this man's presence. "'Knack' was used by my people, too. My grandmother had a knack with pies

and healing herbs. Hers was an enviable set of talents…
thought to be magic by some, God-given by others.
She said she was just born to it. So…are you saying
you believe I have a knack for helping people find
their place…?" Playfully Lotte asked, "Where exactly
is it that you would like to be placed this evening,
Mr. Adams?"

"Dr. Carlotta Jenkins…Lotte, I am exactly where
I want to be. Exactly."

"So am I," she said. Playfully leaning into his
shoulder, she repeated, "So am I.

MR. ADAMS

With most of the guests gone, Mr. Adams relaxed against Lotte's kitchen counter and watched the pianist pack up his sheet music and keyboard. A few of Liz's friends gathered the last of the cups and glasses and placed them in the sink. He could hear Lotte encourage the departing guests to take leftovers along with them. As the last couple collected the party remnants to take downstairs to the trash, it seemed right to stay, to be there with Lotte alone.

Rinsing one final glass, he peered through the window above the sink into the dark garden across the street. His mind wandered lazily to the peas he sowed the previous day. He pictured the seeds under the stillness of the winter earth, waiting. It was early for peas, but he'd soaked them overnight to loosen their crinkled, dried shells and then blanketed them with a thick side-dressing of compost for warmth. *It might work...if there's enough light when the pea shoots begin to show above ground. On second thought,* he wondered, *perhaps I could hasten things along by sprinkling in some worm castings.*

Lotte interrupted his thoughts as she took the glass from his hand for the dishwasher.

"That was a nice party, Lotte," he said, admiring the bend of her body as she closed the dishwasher door and touched the "on" button.

"I love having people here," she responded. The way her eyes met his reassured him. She wanted him to stay. "This was the easiest party I've ever hosted. Liz's friends are gems, so helpful. We've nothing left to do. Thanks to you, too, for everything you've done, John."

"Even Thea's father and mother seemed to enjoy themselves," he observed.

"In-laws," Lotte corrected him. "They're Winn's parents. An interesting couple, it turns out. I don't know why they bug Thea so much. But...families are complicated."

John nodded. Saying anything more was unnecessary. Families...*people* are complicated, indeed. He wondered if he should apologize for the afternoon's misadventure, but stopped short as Lotte moved closer, her face near enough to kiss.

She whispered, "It was a good time, the best in a long time."

He inhaled her scent, a mix of pumpkin pie spices and lavender, and backed away—momentarily frightened by the force of his arousal. Concerned then that his hesitation might be misread, Mr. Adams fumbled to find the words to tell this beautiful, spirited woman what she meant to him. How could he express to her the freedom that had grown inside him since meeting her last spring? It was as if she loosened the crinkled, dried shell of his very self, and years of fear and loneliness had escaped their restraint.

Lotte extricated him from his muddling thoughts with a surprising invitation. "Come, let's go down to the garden." He caught the flash of her coy smile, and before he could respond she was heading to retrieve their coats from her room. Not that he would have objected to any destination she chose to lead him.

When Lotte returned, she was carrying a lantern with a large red bow tied to its handle. She handed him his jacket and a wrapped box to carry. "C batteries," was the only explanation she gave. "Ready?"

For the second time that day, Mr. Adams found himself accompanying Lotte down her flight of stairs—this time, hand-in-hand and at a leisurely pace.

Outside the rain had stopped. Puddles sparkled pinkish-orange in the glow of street lamps. A thick fog from the bay reflected the ambient light, making easy passage of their way through the garden. Lotte led him to the back of the stage. There, she bent down and left the lantern several inches inside the opening where it would be protected from the elements and the views of any unlikely passersby, but obvious to anyone who deliberately tried to enter the space. Mr. Adams handed her the box of batteries and she placed it next to the lamp.

Deeply affected by Lotte's unspoken thoughtfulness, Mr. Adams imagined Jake's solitary pleasure when he found her gift the next morning. "Mrs. Claus, you are something else entirely," he said.

He opened his hand, wordlessly offering to warm her hand in his. She held out both hands and he tucked them into his jacket pockets, bringing the full length of her body against his. He placed his palm against the small of her back and drew her closer.

"Brrr," she said, burying her head into his shoulder.

He found it easy to tell her how much he wanted to kiss her. To his delight, she responded with laughing eyes.

"My dear Mr. Adams—or I mean…John? You are one fast mover. A full year, and already you want a kiss?"

"I do," he said, tipping her chin gently upwards. An inch from her lips, he paused, enjoying the sensation of the soft stream of her exhalation against his face. Inhaling, he closed the distance between them and met her lips for the first time.

It wasn't a long kiss, but more perfect than any of the countless kisses he'd imagined with her. He moved his hand to the nape of Lotte's neck inside her coat and relished the feel of her skin under his fingers. He sighed and closed his eyes. Lotte's lips touched his with such directness…exactly as he hoped they would. He experienced only the tiniest hesitancy from her, a slight pullback and tightening of her neck muscles followed by a palpable release in her body that left him shivering, not from the cold. A brief moment in time, it contained a lifetime promise for him.

"Hmmm…?" he heard her ask.

"Uh-huh," he answered, his eyes closed.

"You okay?"

Mr. Adams opened his eyes and grinned. "Just savoring the moment, 'fast mover' that I am. How about you?"

"Completely okay. Only, didn't want to find you falling asleep." Feeling Lotte's body stiffen, he worried she might not be joking. Had he blown their sublime connection?

"Are you a fast mover?" she whispered. "We don't know anything about each other, do we? I mean in this way...do we? It's been all about Allegra, and ideas and books and politics...and the garden."

He sighed and let his arms drop to his side, freeing her. "Lotte, I am anything but a fast mover. I want you to know me and I want to know you, too." He moved back a few steps so he could lean on the edge of the stage for support, and beckoned, hoping Lotte would follow. She did. Standing next to her, he let the sounds of Christmas Eve fill their silence. He recognized an old recording of Nat King Cole floating from a first-floor window in Lotte's building, "Chestnuts Roasting on an Open Fire." A distant siren wailed, a reminder that all was not easy elsewhere in the city.

He felt from her stillness that Lotte was waiting for him to talk first. Where to start? The sadness after Marjorie and Julia died? The few generous women who, over the years, had tried kindly, but were unsuccessful to draw him out? He'd been such a coward with them, and they each drifted away—disappointed, hurt by his incapacity to carry through. Determined not to repeat this with Lotte, he began. The more he spoke, the closer he felt her presence and the softer the brittle shell enclosing his heart.

"The most courteous thing to do seemed to withdraw into the safety of my solitude. So I didn't return phone calls, that kind of thing," he tried to explain. "But truth is, I felt like I was some kind of death curse.

Why love, when love dies? I was terrified…terrified it would happen again." *Too dramatic?* he worried. He felt over-exposed. Muted and embarrassed, he sought Lotte's eyes and was relieved to find her focused on him without judgment.

She spoke softly. "I know something of that kind of fear."

As Lotte described the sheer pain and emotional upheaval she experienced in the months after learning of Vince's betrayals, Mr. Adams's heart clenched. He wanted to touch her cheek, to hold her tight to him, to comfort her. But he knew instinctively this wasn't what she needed.

"Vince was the first time I'd been head-over-heels in love. I let myself go. As they say, 'a fool in love.'" He sensed Lotte's body sinking and ineffectively wished again that he could help lift her, free her of her grief—but he was immobilized by the weight of his own. "After I learned about all the other women…I found it hard to trust again." He heard her exhale. Mr. Adams let Lotte's rueful words fall into the stillness. He wondered how he could have been so naive as to think that they could put their pasts behind them. Were they both fools to think they could move on?

Then, without warning, laughter surged inside him and erupted. Full, galloping laughter, more tender than bold. Not a thigh-slapping kind of laughter, but no-good-reason, sweet, hopeful elation. Up from the bottom of his belly, melting right through his heart, carrying its own joyful momentum. The laughter of someone who knows better but barrels ahead regardless, daring to meet life face-to-face again.

And there was Lotte, laughing too. The sound was infectious, and he laughed harder, dislodging sharp edges of horrible sorrow. Lotte's cheeks were streaming with tears. His too. They fell, doubled up against each other, laughter and tears mixing without sense.

Finally able to speak, he said with mock seriousness, "So here we are, fifty-somethings literally in the dark. And I'm afraid to kiss you again because…" he sputtered with laughter, "Because you'll…die."

"Which I surely will," came Lotte's gleeful reply.

As if it were the most hilarious thing in the world, Mr. Adams continued, "I'm afraid to be happy because…death will rip it away."

"No doubt about it," hooted Lotte. "And me? I'm scared you'll betray me."

Mr. Adams tried to stop then because the thought of hurting Lotte was too awful to imagine, but his laughter was uncontrollable. "It's inevitable…I will. Guaranteed."

"Yes," shouted Lotte, gripping both his hands. "Of course you will. And I will betray you too. In countless ways…"

He brought Lotte's hands gently to his lips, one by one. Her face close enough for him to breathe in her breath, Mr. Adams kissed her again. This time for a very long time.

When their lips finally separated, Lotte's face was so close he couldn't focus. Everything he saw was Lotte, and he drank in the sight.

He held his breath and whispered, "That may have been the bravest thing I've ever done."

Lotte whispered back, "Me? Hoping for another kiss…is the bravest thing I've ever done."

Barely aware of what he was saying, he asked, "Lotte? Carlotta? Will you marry me?"

He heard Lotte chuckle, but she didn't move away. In fact, she nuzzled closer into his embrace. "Not a fast mover, Mr. Adams…? Precipitous would be more accurate. One date, two kisses, and the next moment…a proposal of marriage?"

Mr. Adams leaned his forehead to touch hers, lightheartedly enjoying how they balanced against each other for a moment. Then, matching Lotte's mischievous tone, he made his case.

"See, I'd like to sleep over sometimes and have pancakes in the morning. Allegra said I could, if we were married."

"Did she now? That little girl…" He heard Lotte slowly repeat his question, "Will I marry you…?" She turned her face away and he caught his breath. When she looked back at him her eyes lit with promise. "How 'bout you just keep asking...?"

Their lips met for a third time. Closing his eyes, he floated into a field of swirling purple and green light and rested in the delicious softness of her lips.

THE END

A BRIEF LIST OF
COMMUNITY GARDENS AND
URBAN AGRICULTURE RESOURCES

- American Community Gardening Association | *www.communitygarden.org*
- USDA Office of Urban Agriculture and Innovative Production | *www.usda.gov/topics/urban*
- National Sustainable Agriculture Coalition re: USDA's Office of Urban Agriculture and Innovative Production | *sustainableagriculture.net/blog/a-look-at-the-office-of-urban-agriculture-and-innovative-production*
- EPA Resources about Brownfields and Urban Agriculture | *www.epa.gov/brownfields/resources-about-brownfields-and-urban-agriculture*
- Green Pals Community Garden Statistics 2023 | *gardenpals.com/community-garden*

- Smithsonian Gardens Short History of Community Gardening in the US | *communityofgardens.si.edu/exhibits/show/historycommunitygardens/intro*
- United Nations Food and Agriculture Organization | *www.fao.org/home/en*
- *Farm City: The Education of an Urban Farmer* by Novella Carpenter
- Vermiculture in the City: Small-Scale Composting—Uncle Jim's Worm Farm | *unclejimswormfarm.com/small-scale-composting-worms-vermiculture-city*
- Worm Composting: Complete Beginner's Guide (7 Step Process) | *www.planetnatural.com/worm-composting*

Any Google search will yield bountiful information about your own city's urban farms and community gardens, including municipal policies, how-to tips, advocacy groups, and more to help you find neighbors who share your passion.

Because of my own roots in these two special organizations, I include them here:

- City Sprouts, Omaha Nebraska Nebraska
- Southside Community Land Trust, Providence Rhode Island

ACKNOWLEDGMENTS

Credit goes first to my parents for teaching me about the magic of gardening. One autumn day my father dug a 4-foot square just outside the fence of his own large vegetable garden in our backyard. There he instructed me how to plant daffodil bulbs. We covered the scabby dead-looking lumps with a deep layer of soil to protect them from the Connecticut winter freeze. It was to be my garden he explained, though at the time I don't recall feeling much impressed by this patch of dirt. Of course those of you who have planted bulbs know the amazing surprise he had in mind for his little girl when Spring brought forth a dazzling yellow display of sweet-scented flowers, from *my* garden. I picked every one of the blossoms and presented them proudly to my mother. Down to my toes I can still feel her delight.

Fast forward forty years to a Spring morning in

my own large garden, in Omaha Nebraska. Despondent, I'd sought solace in pulling weeds from the cool ground. In the previous two weeks, three drive-by shootings a few blocks away from our street had my neighbors and me reeling with grief and confusion. I was at a loss for what to do. "Transitional" was how city planners described our part of Omaha in those years. As the city stretched its boundaries westward into farmland, our beautiful tree-lined neighborhood of stately homes with wide porches and large backyards was falling into neglect. After the murders, things felt headed from bad to worse, with little hope for an upswing in fortunes. I credit unseen forces in my garden that morning for the idea that led to what happened next.

Everything changed for the better when neighbors came together to clear trash, child-high weeds and mounds of rubble from a vacant lot where a teen-aged boy had been killed. Strangers became friends and sunflowers bloomed in the hell-strip next to the sidewalk. By summer's end we were wealthy in tomatoes, zucchinis, and pride. We named our garden City Sprouts.

Since then I've had the opportunity to witness the remarkable healing power of many community gardens around the world. The Sweet Folly of Hope is my humble and grateful bow to the inspiring work of city people who are working in concert with the earth to transform lives and deepen lasting connections through gardening.

Heartfelt thanks to Helen Glasgow and Roz Reed as well. Lotte's character is drawn from these two wonderful women who profoundly influenced my life in important ways. Unfortunately they are no longer with us. But it is my fondest hope that they would recognize themselves in Lotte's wisdom, kindness, clarity, and in her courage to love, no matter what.

The first draft of the novel was born over three months in the solitude of Mary Power and Bill Dietrich's forest cabin on the Eel River, north of San Francisco. I had little experience with writing fiction but the story kept unfolding and I tried my best to keep up. Later, brilliant short story writer and writing teacher, Hester Kaplan pointed out among other technicalities that my prose would improve if I kept to only one point of view at a time. Who knew? Novelist Taylor Polites' insightful comments from a close reading of the manuscript encouraged a total revision. Only after retirement was this possible, and more significantly, only with help from my good friend Carol Scott, a writer's dream of an editor. The final draft came together at last in Linda Pololi and Athanasius Anagnostou's tranquil home overlooking Almy Creek Marsh in Rhode Island.

My sincere appreciation goes to Sarah Zachs,

Penney Stein, Carol Faye, Cheryl Zimmerman, Ellen Bar-Zimmer, Sally Rotenberg and Lauren Ruo for reading early rough drafts, and to Janice Newman for help with the book cover design. Thanks also to Betsy Johnson, pioneer community gardener and member of the American Community Gardening Association, for her encouraging feedback.

My brother Rush Brown provided the charming sketch of a garden arbor to mark the change of seasons throughout the book. The team at Stillwater River Publications has guided me throughout the publishing and distribution process with expertise and respect. Leslie McGee's patient guidance steered me through the mysteries of social media.

Diane Gillespie, my writing partner for more than thirty years, deserves my deepest gratitude. How many drafts did Diane slog through, her confidence never ceasing that one day I'd eventually finish.

May gardens everywhere nourish our precious world with the sweet folly of hope.

ABOUT THE AUTHOR

KATHERINE has firsthand experience in the healing power of community gardens. In 1995 she founded City Sprouts, an urban agriculture project in Omaha NE. Inspired by the immediate and far-reaching effects she observed when people gather to grow food together in the city, Katherine eventually left her academic career (health policy and ethics) to promote urban agriculture as a potent agent for positive community, environmental and economic change. She consults and publishes on the subject.

Katherine lives in Providence, Rhode Island, where

before retiring, she helped Southside Community Land Trust develop new gardens and farms for hundreds of families to grow healthy food and community. A Buddhist, she studies and teaches in the New Kadampa Tradition. She loves to garden, swim, laugh, and share the joy of reading and writing.